waiting for elvis

waiting for elvis

A NOVEL

david elias

COTEAU BOOKS

© David Elias, 2008.

All rights reserved. No part of this publication may be reproduced, stored in a retrieval system or transmitted, in any form or by any means, without the prior written consent of the publisher or a licence from The Canadian Copyright Licensing Agency (Access Copyright). For an Access Copyright licence, visit www.accesscopyright.ca or call toll free to 1-800-893-5777.

This is a work of fiction. Names, characters, places, and incidents either are the product of the author's imagination or are used fictitiously. Any resemblance to actual persons, living or dead, is coincidental.

Edited by Edna Alford.
Book and cover design by Duncan Campbell.
Cover image: "Booth Seating at Diner," by WireImageStock/Masterfile.

Printed and bound in Canada at Friesens.
This book is printed o 100% recycled paper.

Library and Archives Canada Cataloguing in Publication

Elias, David H., 1949-
    Waiting for Elvis : a novel / David Elias.

ISBN 978-1-55050-394-4

I. Title.

PS8559.L525W35 2008   C813'.54   C2008-903933-5

10 9 8 7 6 5 4 3 2 1

COTEAU BOOKS
2517 Victoria Ave.
Regina, Saskatchewan
Canada S4P 0T2

AVAILABLE IN CANADA & THE US FROM
Fitzhenry & Whiteside
195 Allstate Parkway
Markham, ON, Canada, L3R 4T8

The publisher gratefully acknowledges the financial assistance of the Saskatchewan Arts Board, the Canada Council for the Arts, the Government of Canada through the Book Publishing Industry Development Program (BPIDP), Association for the Export of Canadian Books, and the City of Regina Arts Commission, for its publishing program.

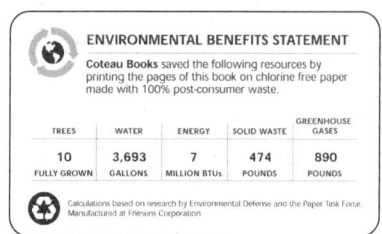

*This book is dedicated
to the memory of Gibb Nordin,
who loved words.*

What's madness but nobility of soul
At odds with circumstance? The day's on fire!
— ROETHKE, *In A Dark Time*

prologue

THE VIOLENT CONCUSSION OF THE STEEL FIST WAKES Sal into total silence. Paralyzed, unable to turn even his eyes from side to side, to move even the tiniest muscle – yet incredibly alive – like some insect on a branch, all he can do is lie there and listen. All the traffic sounds have stopped. Impossible, complete silence.

Sal is alive beyond the possibility of quiet death, or safety or reason, alive beyond all sensibility. Like quivering flesh of fresh meat born out of blood, hot blood, fire eyes, tingle skin, crackle and snake slithering restlessness, all in a black bed, a black bed that will never move cannot move cannot be made thin enough to fit between the wall and the door so far so far from the end of the bed where voices never comfort but shout and wail. They could never be a comfort.

Sounds seeping through the cracks to find him in his bed. The tick tick ticking of the big brown clock scolding him from the kitchen wall – tsk tsk tsking him. The slap slap slap of Clothespin Harry's hands on Rosa's naked flesh. The knack, knack, knack of the old oak headboard against the plaster wall. The grunt of Harry's effort – all of these come through the cracks in the warped door that won't close all the way.

waiting for elvis

Lying in his hammock, strung up between the pines, Sal becomes aware of the first few sounds sneaking up out of the silence in which they've become embedded. The rustle chirp and tingle of the forest – mixed in, somehow, with the tick tick ticking of the big brown clock on the kitchen wall. Louder now, they grow until the screaming buzz of a billion insects above and below and just behind his back makes Sal's skin crawl. And then the highway, hissing at him again until it becomes a roar, pounding into his ears, all the sounds bleeding into it, disappearing into it, into the endless waves of traffic noise that wash in through the pines.

Slowly, each tick a thousand years, using all of his willpower, Sal is able to make himself move – first his eyes, then a slight turn of his head from side to side, then a fingertip, and so on until he thaws out, thaws back into something that can move and breathe. And as he does, the insect buzz and the other night noises subside, the tick tick ticking of the big clock the last thing to slip under the hum hiss and crackle scrub of the traffic a hundred yards away.

Sal uses every muscle he can control to fling himself violently out of the hammock, lands in a heap on the forest floor, nothing to break his fall but pine needles. Then he's up, crawling across the prickly orange carpet on his hands and knees, clawing at the needles, letting them pierce the tips of his curved fingers, the sheaths of his thick sweating palms. Wailing like a child he's up and running now, to a place deeper into the woods where, hanging from ropes and chains and odd pieces of electrical wiring are countless pieces of metal and glass, plastic and rubber. Sal gets up a good head of steam before he runs headlong into the middle of them, staggers and weaves like a fullback, two arms clutching his great bulky coat – the coat he never takes off – close around him. It gives him some protection now, but also adds momentum as he throws himself against a heavy truck bumper with a grunt and thud of flesh into unforgiving steel. Lunges against a driveshaft, the sharp edge where it snapped slashing into his

waiting for elvis

forehead. He runs on. Puts a shoulder into a pickup hood. Drives his chest into a dirty black quarter panel. Crashes headlong into a car door and shatters the glass into a million pieces. Runs and tackles until all that pain and chaos on the outside begins to resemble a little of what's happening to his insides. Runs until he feels himself losing consciousness. And only then can he stop. Stop now. Sway like a sleepy drunk, gulping air, sweat soaked, eyes wide. Sway in time with a shiny hubcap that hangs before his face like a warped mirror. Look into it at his bizarre reflection, nose big as a foot, gash across his forehead bleeding fiercely, cheekbone bruised and purple, lip cut and swollen, crushed ear dripping blood.

chapter one

THE PLACE ISN'T MUCH TO LOOK AT FROM THE ROAD. A small square-frame building put together out of spruce studs and plywood. There's a sign across the front that reads "Betty's Diner – Home of the Giant Cinnamon Bun." Arty, Betty's husband, scrawled the letters out across two four-by-eight sheets of plywood he'd framed together, painted them green against a white background. Betty thought it was just about the ugliest thing she'd ever seen. She wanted a fancier sign but Arty said it would do just fine so long as it was big enough to draw attention from the road. Said there were more important things to spend the money on, money he'd saved up trucking before he talked Betty into buying the place.

"But it's in the middle of nowhere," she protested when he took her out to see it for the first time.

"That's the beauty," said Arty. That was his answer for a lot of things. "No competition." He used it on her again when she protested about the gaudy sign.

"Green?" she said when she saw what he'd concocted. "Christ, Arty, it's so goddamn ugly nobody in their right mind would stop here to get something to eat."

waiting for elvis

"That's the beauty," Arty shot back. "Truckers'll know this is no fancy-pants place and come right in." Arty used to be a trucker himself, so he always pulls that out like a gun, too, every time there's something to be settled. "I know truckers. They don't need the sizzle as long as you give them the steak."

Betty didn't think much of his logic. She was interested from the start in attracting more than just truckers if they were going to make a go of the place. She let Arty win out about the sign, though, not because she didn't think she could put up enough of a fight to make him give in, but because money was tight and she thought they could always get a proper sign later.

That was seven years ago. It's still up there, not quite straight anymore after one of the boards rotted and some of the nails let go. The green letters have faded to the colour of oatmeal, barely readable against the chipped white paint covering the plywood. Lately business is better than ever, though. The truckers, especially, seem to be coming in more than they usually do. Staying longer. Betty thinks it must have something to do with all the talk about twinning the highway further out of Winnipeg, all the way through to Kenora, some say. So far there hasn't been anything official. No suits coming around. No paperwork. But it's only a matter of time.

"Saw the surveyors are out where the divided ends the other day," says Harvey. He's one of the regulars. Comes in three or four times a week. He drives a Greyhound bus and his trips take him past the diner on his way in and out of Winnipeg. Mostly he stops by when he's empty – usually heading out to pick up a load of seniors and take them into the city from Kenora or Dryden for a day of gambling at the casino. He's up at one of the stools that run along the counter, talking to Arty through the serving window. "Pretty soon it'll be bulldozers and scrapers. Mark my word." Twinning the highway through to Kenora means the end of the diner. The corridor they slash through the rock and bush will cut right through the place.

"Take 'em about five minutes to level this place on their way through," says Arty. He's cutting up the clubhouse sandwich he just made for Harvey and piling up the plate with fries. He puts the plate up on the ledge of the window for Betty to pass to him. Arty does the short-order cooking, burgers and fries mostly, and the usual assortment of sandwiches. Betty waits the tables, but she also does the real cooking – makes the soup first thing every morning, throws in the roasts of ham and beef. Cooks the chickens and turkeys. Things like that.

"Somebody oughta do something," says Harvey.

"Like what?" says Arty.

"Talk to the guy in charge. Minister of whatever. Get him to see reason."

"Wouldn't do any good. Nobody over there gives two shits about a little place like this. They got bigger fish to fry."

"Well, all I can say is it's a goddamn shame."

That's the way they go at it, day after day. Arty and people like Harvey. Betty tunes it out most of the time. She doesn't feel a lot of anxiety about losing the place. Driving forty-five minutes through nothing but spruce and birch and bog to get here every morning when they could just as well let it go and set up another diner next to the highway closer to town. The government will have to give them a fair price and they can use the money to start up the new one. Get a proper sign. Something they can be proud of. She's thinking a bulldozer might be the best thing that ever happened.

Better yet, they could get out of the business altogether. Sell the house in town, maybe move to the coast. Betty's always wanted to live on the coast. Might be just the thing Tony needs as well, to get him away from those so-called friends of his. The ones he's been hanging around with ever since Arty let him have the motorcycle. It's an old Harley Davidson Arty used to take her for rides on back when they first met. Back when they couldn't keep their hands off each other. It sat in the back of the garage for so long Betty forgot all about it.

"It'll give him something to do," said Arty. "Keep him out of trouble." Tony's been getting into one kind of trouble or another as long as Betty can remember. She didn't want him to have the bike at all. Knew it would all go bad somehow.

"You've seen the bunch in town who ride those things," said Betty. "You want him in with that crowd? Besides, that thing is a piece of junk. Probably needs a lot of work."

"That's the beauty," said Arty. "It'll take him all summer just to get the damn thing on the road. If he's lucky." But the day after Arty gave it to him two guys from town showed up on bikes of their own. They were older. Rough looking. Between the three of them they had Arty's old motorcycle up and running in two days. The idea that Tony would help out around the diner as part of the bargain hasn't worked out either. It's always the same. He and Arty find something to get into a fight about and Tony storms out the door. Gets on that damn motorcycle and rides off. Betty hates the sound of it now. The loud vulgar gargle of it. Wonders if maybe she always did. It sounds so angry. Arty never does much to try and stop him. Betty can sense he doesn't really want Tony around the place. They don't see much of him these days. He stays out most of the night, sleeps all day. Most of the time when she and Arty leave for the diner in the morning he hasn't come in yet, and by the time they get back in the evening, he's long gone.

"Saw that same guy up along the highway again today," says Harvey to Arty. "The one you said came in here the other day." Betty can see Arty bristle, throw her a quick glance from behind the window. "He's out there. Prowling around next to the highway."

"He's not hurting anyone," says Betty.

"Can't figure out what the hell he's up to," says Harvey. "Must have a place up there in the woods somewhere. Mosquitoes and black flies must be eating him alive."

"No skin off my nose," says Arty.

"It was you that talked to him. Isn't that right, Betty?" says Harvey.

"That's right."

"Never said a word. Isn't that what you said?" He looks over at Arty, then back at Betty. "What the hell did he want anyway?"

"Same as you," says Betty, trying to keep an even tone. "Some company."

"Looks to me like he's been out there a long time. You never know about a guy like that."

"A guy like what?" says Betty. She can't quite understand why she feels the need to defend any of it.

"You know, a guy that won't talk to you."

Betty thinks Harvey could just as easily be talking about Arty. She can't remember the last time they had a real conversation. Thinks that maybe they never have.

"Better that way," says Arty. "Probably wouldn't make any sense anyway. Crazy as a bedbug, if you ask me."

It happened in one of those rare times when she was alone in the place. Arty wasn't back from picking up supplies in the city and the last trucker of the day had just turned back onto the highway into the dusk. She was getting ready to close up when she saw someone emerge from the woods and cross the parking lot. She could make out the husky figure of a man through the window. Even under the massive coat he was wearing she could see that he had a muscular build, an athletic walk. She thought of running over to lock the door, but there was nothing of menace in his movement. An element of stealth, yes. Perhaps even a hint of the fugitive. But nothing in the way he carried himself that made her want to run over and bolt the door. And so she let him approach until she could make out his face a little better. He was a man of uncertain age, with a wild head of hair and a handsome ruggedness in his features. He had an untamed look about him, but not the kind she'd seen in other strangers. There was more there of fear than danger.

Then she thought perhaps he had been hurt. That maybe there'd been another horrific pileup where the divided ended. That he was the victim of a crash and had wandered away from the scene of the accident. Maybe he's in shock, she thought. He certainly had that look about him. Of someone who had no idea where he was. Who he was. And so she opened the door and went out into the cool evening air – the air that always had the smell of the wilderness about it – toward him.

"Are you alright?" she said.

The man stopped. Gave no answer. Pulled the greatcoat around him. Looked at her as though she were a fire he wanted to warm himself next to. But also, as though he was afraid of fire.

"Can I help you?"

He seemed unable to speak. Or perhaps only unwilling. She couldn't decide which. They were closer now and she tried to see into his eyes, but he would not allow it. Averted his gaze. There was a fierce timidity about him. She felt it. Felt the depth of it. He might be a runaway, she thought. Someone who wandered out here from the city. Escaped from one of those places where they keep people like him. People who need looking after. He certainly had that about him, too. The look of someone who needed looking after. Someone who spent a long time being neglected. Perhaps abused. Somebody must have hurt him, she thought. Or maybe he'd hurt himself.

"Come in," she said. She reached for his arm. He let her take it. "Come in and sit down."

She led him into the diner then, the way one human being leads another when both are in need of something – the one to offer, the other to accept. She sat him down in one of the booths, watched him put his hands up on the surface of the Formica tabletop, as though he were waiting for a manicure.

"You must be hungry," she said. "Why don't I fix you something to eat? I'll be right back," she said, and disappeared into the kitchen. She'd turned off the grill and the deep fryers for the night, but she warmed some leftover soup and made him a roast beef sandwich. While she prepared the food she watched him through the serving window, saw the way he sat straight, eyes wandering around the interior of the diner, like someone in a museum. Everything seemed to be a wonder to him. New. Strange.

She brought the food out to him and set it down on the table in front of him. He looked up at her then, just for a second, and she saw his eyes up close for the first time. Saw how deep and green they were. Saw the flecks of blue and orange around the

waiting for elvis

edges. There was an intensity there she'd never seen before. As if he were trying to tell her something so intently that his eyes might burst into flame. Something of suffering. Of the memory of suffering.

She put her hand out and placed it lightly on his shoulder. At first, under her hand, it seemed to her that he must be made of solid stone. The muscle and bone there as rigid as rock. He's as tight as a drum, she thought. Frightened out of his wits. Then she felt something else coming up through the tips of her fingers. Something like a vibration. Thought she heard it, too, like a soft buzzing in her ears. His whole body humming.

"It's alright," she said.

He did not pull himself away from her touch, but neither did he surrender to it. A kind of quiet reluctance. Not quick and hurtful and confusing, the way it had always been with Tony. From the very first, her son had always resisted physical contact. Made it clear he wanted nothing to do with her. Tensed up and writhed away from her reach in a way that made her feel she'd done something wrong. Violated him somehow. All through his infancy, his early childhood, she'd lain awake at night, wondering why her own child cringed at the touch of her. Arty wasn't around much back then. He was still trucking in those days, but it was always the same when he was home and she tried to talk to him about their son's troubling behaviour.

"He treats me like I'm poison," said Betty.

"You're exaggerating."

"Easy for you to say. You're not here to see it."

"Here we go again," Arty would say.

"Treats you the same way. Like a stranger."

"He'll grow out of it."

"Grow out of it? Christ, Arty."

"Do we have to go through this every time I come home?"

"I've been thinking maybe we should get someone to take a look at him."

"What the hell does that mean?"

"You know. A doctor. A specialist."

waiting for elvis

"What kind of specialist? What are you getting at?"

"Someone who knows about that kind of thing."

"You mean a shrink. Is that it? Jesus, Betty, now you want to turn him into a nutcase."

"I'm not saying that. I'm just saying we have to do something. Maybe if you spent more time with him, you'd see it too."

"Okay, so I stay home and you go out and drive the rig. Is that the idea?"

Betty was pretty sure she could learn to drive the rig as well as Arty, but she knew it would never work the other way around, and so she said, "When you're home, I mean. Maybe if you made a little more of an effort."

"I come in off the road and I'm tired, Betty. The way I am right now. Too goddamn tired to listen to any more of this bullshit."

It always went like that and nothing ever changed, until one day Tony was sprouting fuzzy hairs on his chin and stealing Arty's dirty magazines and it was too late. It was as if a young man had been thrust into their midst who wanted nothing to do with them. Who wished he could go home to his real mother and father. Betty woke up one morning from another troubled sleep and realized that it was she who felt as if she'd been adopted. That she was part of a family that had nothing to do with warmth or blood.

Betty sat across from the stranger and watched as he looked down at the bowl of soup, put his nose over it, took in the smell of it. The heat. Watched as he picked up the spoon and started in. Not fiercely, not ravenously. He was clearly hungry, took in the nourishment with great intent and purpose, and yet there was a certain grace about it. A certain innocence. Nothing like the truckers she was used to serving. They ate their meals with a kind of grudging indulgence, used the consumption of food as a way of putting off their loneliness and boredom. A way to buy some time before they would have to get back into their rigs and give themselves over once more to the traffic and the noise, the cigarettes and amphetamines.

waiting for elvis

She watched him take up the glass of milk she'd brought and drink the contents down in a series of deep guttural swallows that were audible from where she sat. Saw his Adam's apple work up and down along his muscular neck under the growth of stubble there. There were signs of recent injury – an angry red scar on his forehead, another on his lip and on one ear – but they were almost healed over now. If he was an accident victim it must have been a while ago. But then, she thought, if he's lost his memory there's no telling how long he's been out there. She checked his wrists for a hospital band and saw none. Examined his clothes. The heavy coat had every pocket stuffed to bursting. There were dark stains in a couple of places that looked like they might be dried blood.

And then, for the first time, she took in the smell of him. Sweat and dirt. And something else. Something familiar. The last time she'd smelled that odour was back when she was still Elizabeth and her father had come home from someplace far away, a stranger in a uniform the colour of this man's coat. She was wearing a new pink dress with puffed sleeves, and her mother was motioning for her to step into the room, the kitchen, and allow herself to be picked up by a man she did not remember and to sit on his lap. That was where she'd smelled it before. It was the smell of combat. Of blood and war and death. And the look of this stranger was the same. Something in him of the soldier. The same fatigue she'd seen in her father's features. The memory of something. The need to feel safe again. What kind of a war has this man been in, Betty wondered. Who has he been at war with?

"Is there someone I can call?" she said when he'd finished the last morsel of the cinnamon bun she'd brought him for dessert. He looked up at her as if she had asked him the most difficult question he'd ever heard. He understands me, she thought. He knows every word I'm saying to him.

"Are you able to speak?" she said.

He looked away, out the window, and then she was looking, too, because a pickup truck was slowing down on the highway

waiting for elvis

and getting ready to turn in. It was Arty. The man looked back at her for a moment, showed a new kind of fear in his eyes she hadn't seen before. A new level of alarm. Of agitation. Arty might just as well be coming there to kill him. He was that terrified. And then, before she could even reach out her hand to him, say a single word of comfort, of reassurance, he was up from the booth, striding through the door, across the parking lot. And then he was gone, disappeared back into the spruce and birch and poplar.

When Arty walked into the diner a minute later with a cardboard box under his arm and stopped, let the door close behind him, Betty froze. She was half up out of the booth, unsure now whether to get up or sit back down. The moment seemed encased in amber, the two of them smothered in pale yellow light. It had all been so bright a minute ago, and now it seemed to her that nothing much could happen. Things stayed that way for what seemed like a long time. Arty standing just inside the door with the cardboard box in his arms. Betty half up out of the booth, leaning over the table, unable to move. Then the world started up again and she heard Arty say, "Who the hell was that?"

"I don't know," she said.

"Where'd he come from?"

"He just wandered in," said Betty.

"What the hell was he doing here?"

"I'm telling you, Arty, I don't know."

"Jesus, he didn't try anything did he?"

"No."

Betty picked up the dishes and cutlery and headed for the kitchen. Arty followed her with the box still in his arms.

"What'd he say his name was?"

"He didn't." She was looking down into the plate, at the swirls of leftover syrup from the cinnamon bun.

"Didn't tell you his name?"

"No." Some kind of pattern, there on the plate. Some kind of design.

Arty put the box down on the countertop. "How the hell did he get in here?"

"He just walked in. Same as anybody else." It wasn't possible. Just her imagination.

"Goddammit, Betty, you're always talking about attracting a better class of customer and then you let a guy like that come in here."

Betty was still looking down at the swirls of cinnamon syrup on the plate.

"If he tries to come in here again you call the cops," said Arty.

Maybe it was just a bunch of squiggles that didn't mean anything. Maybe she was the one imposing meaning on them because she wanted to. Needed to.

"Goddammit, Betty, are you listening to me?"

She looked up at Arty and saw his features cloud over with that familiar look he sometimes got. When she'd scared him a little. "Look," she said. "He was harmless. Nothing happened. Just some lost soul who wandered in here for something to eat. That's all. He's gone now, so let's drop it and go home."

Betty knew she had nothing to feel guilty about, and yet she felt the unexplainable sensation of having been ravaged somehow – not by the physicality of the stranger, not by his eyes, which would haunt her tonight when she tried to get to sleep. And it wasn't the way his Adam's apple moved when he drank the glass of milk, or the look of his great gnarled hand when he picked up the roast beef sandwich. It wasn't the reddened scar, shiny and new across his forehead. No, it was his silence that had invaded her. The feel of it, even now, deep in her chest, in the pit of her stomach.

Something about that. The openness of it. The space. A space she'd never been inside before. Where a person who could speak – she was absolutely certain of that – chose not to. And the reason, she knew, as surely as she had ever known anything in her life, was a wellspring of suffering. She'd seen that much in his eyes. In the starbursts of blue and orange that flickered there. A place of sadness and tragedy. A dark and terrible and unspeakable place – but a place she nevertheless wanted to travel to.

"Well what the hell did he want?"

That, Betty thought, as she took the plate over to the sink to rinse it, was the first question Arty had asked that made any sense.

"I don't know," she said. "I don't know anything about him." And just before she turned on the hot water and held the plate underneath it, she looked once more at the swirls there – swore she could make out three distinct letters. s – a – l.

They closed up after that and made the drive back to Hayden, but all the way home there was an edge to Arty's silence, to Betty's. She couldn't stop thinking about the letters on the plate. Couldn't understand why there was something about them that seemed familiar to her. And she couldn't help thinking maybe she'd lied to Arty. That maybe, in some unexplainable way, it was possible she already knew more about the silent man who'd sat across the table from her than she did about the man sitting next to her right now.

chapter two

SAL AT THE EDGE OF THE FOREST, LOOKING OVER FOUR lanes of streaming cars and trucks in a river of incessant noise that never stops. He can taste the nasty aftershock of the steel fist in his mouth, dried to a gritty harshness at the back of his tongue. It came last night and tore him out of his sleep. Left behind this ache that numbs his skull. The same skidding out of control. Rubber bruising asphalt. Ripped metal. Torn flesh. The quick and savage impact of his own mind crashing.

Not more than an hour after sunrise and already it's hot. Today will be like every other day in August. Cars will overheat. Truck tires will burst. Air conditioners will fail. But nothing will stop the flow. Nothing. Not even death. Death is just part of the energy. Sal's seen it. Heard it. Mangled metal. Tangled bodies. Blood. Wail and moan. Then tow trucks and police and ambulances for an hour or two while the river flows around the death. No crosses here to bear witness. None needed. Nobody on this highway is from around here. No one would care. When Sal stands next to it like this he can feel the madness of it. The heartbeat blood rush gush gulped air wide-eyed crush of its insistence. The single-minded lunacy of all those drivers in a great, solitary procession of isolation.

waiting for elvis

They make a great and terrible noise, all of them. All those engines and tires concussing the air, pushing everything out of the way. Their inertia curses combustion at the air, swears fumes at the sky, the trees, the sun. Chokes hope out of anything close enough to fall under the cloak of its unrelenting promise. Never to rest. Never to sleep. Like the inertia that builds up sometimes inside Sal's head. Goes on for so long the only thing that can stop the speeding rush of it is the crash of the steel fist.

It's different where the railroad line runs through the Shield, a mile or so to the north, quiet and unseen. There, it is mostly silence. Only now and then the thunder and wind of its purpose revealed in one seamless line of noise and chaos. Sometimes a long line of freight cars, bound for Thunder Bay. Sometimes a slick column of passenger cars, quick and neat as they slip through the wilderness, people like cut-outs at the windows. Then back to silence. Walk a mile off the highway in the other direction and it's the river. A glossy ribbon of water where nothing disturbs the silence but river animals, otters and ducks and deer come to drink. A canoe now and then that Sal always lets slip by. Stays far enough in the woods so there's no chance they'll spot him.

But the highway is different. Today, like every other day, its fury will soak up the quiet like a long, dirty ribbon of sponge. Suck up all other sound. Sal spends his days here, alongside it. Walking next to it. Some days he hums along with it, quietly. The whine and moan of it. Sings out loud and hard because that's not like talking. Not like cold hard words at all. Mimics the howl and screech of the big rigs. On special days he can find the pitch of the highway. Sing above it. Below. Harmonize with the chaos. Find the damned and muted symphony hidden inside it. On a day like that Sal can filter out the hiss and crackle, gurgle and groan. Make a sigh that turns into a note, that becomes a melody.

Most days, though, it exists as a silent roar in his ears, the kind he can only hear with a conscious effort. Like the tick tick ticking of the big brown clock on the kitchen wall back home.

Sal remembers how the sound of it would disappear, from always being there, into the background. How it got covered over by the other noises of the day, so that he was unaware of it until it resurfaced again at night, when it was quiet, and he was moments from sleep. He would conjure it up then – the sound of the ticking – drag it up out of his subconscious, just to make sure that it was still there. When he finally heard the familiar tick tick ticking he could relax. Stop thinking about it. But the moment he did, the sound would disappear again, and he'd have to start over.

It's the same with the highway sounds. When Sal is up in his hammock, strung up between the pines, waiting for sleep, he sometimes thinks they must really have stopped. Then he has to listen hard until the noise lets him know it's still there and he can relax. But then it disappears again and he has to start from the beginning. Nights like that the steel fist is close. Hovers. Waits. He becomes trapped in his own carousel of logic and maybe there's no sleep at all. No rest. No escape from the torture of endless repetition, the tyranny that brutalizes and yet sustains him, keeps him alive.

Sunday afternoon. Clothespin Harry stretched out, back turned, snoring on the long wooden bench under the big clock. The kitchen radio on the other side of the room turned down as far as it will go. The tick tick ticking of the big clock on the wall. Sal crossing the kitchen behind his mother, the keys to Harry's pickup truck clutched in her hand. They've waited until he's good and asleep on the wooden bench. He always sleeps in his greasy coveralls, his broad back turned toward them, the shiny fabric stretching to a glossy finish with each deep breath. Tiptoe across the kitchen, heading for the door, one behind the other, like cartoon criminals.

When Rosa thinks she detects any restlessness in Harry's shoulders, some irregularity in his breathing, she puts a hand out behind her, a signal for them to freeze. Then they have to wait, immobile, like convicts caught in a searchlight, and wait for the sound of his deep, even breathing to resume. Harry takes an enormous breath, pulls in so much air the seams of his coveralls squeak under the

waiting for elvis

strain, ready to pop, the shiny fabric the only thing that keeps his lungs from bursting. He holds the air in his lungs, trapped, suspended, for what seems like a full minute. Sal wants to believe Clothespin Harry has stopped breathing. Has taken in one last enormous breath and just stopped. But then he releases it with such a massive sigh — a sigh so heavy, so long and deep — that the entire house and all its contents seem to collapse with it.

And then simply starts in breathing even and steady again, so Rosa signals that it's alright for them to proceed. When they're finally out of the house and safely on their way there's such a sense of relief that it makes them both a little giddy. Rosa's plan is for the two of them to drive across the line and into town in Harry's pickup and catch the matinee movie at the Walhalla Theatre to see Elvis. She saw something in the newspaper Harry left on the kindling box last night and figured it out, just like she'll figure out quick enough how to handle the pickup truck even though she's never driven it before. Doesn't even have a license. Somehow she learns it right then, right there, because there isn't anything else for her to do. She even knows enough to take the pickup out of gear and let it coast down out of the yard before she turns the engine over.

By the time they make it into town they find things to laugh about that wouldn't be funny any other time.

"Oh, oh," Rosa says. "Traffic jam."

They're pulled up at a stop sign. There are only two cars in the intersection.

"Rush hour," says Sal. They cackle and snort.

"Fish," says Sal after they've parked Clothespin Harry's pickup and are walking up the sidewalk on their way to the theatre. A man with an enormous mouth and bulging eyes has just walked past them.

"Tuna," Rosa says, opening and closing her mouth.

"Bass." Sal makes swimming motions with his arms. They laugh until Sal's throat hurts, until Rosa has to wipe the tears from her eyes.

But the best part of the whole afternoon is when they leave the bright sunshine of the street for the dim interior of the theatre. It's *such a friendly darkness in the carpeted lobby. So welcoming. Rosa pays with ten dollars she stole out of Harry's wallet the night before. If he finds out, there'll be a big hurt, but maybe he won't miss it.*

After they buy popcorn and candy bars, it's even darker when they go in through the swinging doors and find a place to sit down. And then darker again as the lights dim for the start of the movie. The darkness is so delicious Sal wants to swallow it up with his chocolate bar. Sal in a plush red velvet chair. His mother next to him. Her perfume mixed in with the smell of popcorn, her shoulders leaning back against the red velvet. Waiting. Waiting for Elvis.

A low rumble of the curtains pulling apart. The first few flickers of light on the screen and then letters as big as school desks pushing out at them announcing the COMING ATTRACTIONS. A cartoon in which Baby Huey, enormous and idiotic, falls out of the window and lands on the crooks. The world news with Walter Cronkite, his voice a little too baritone, a little too urgent, a little frightening. Tanks and planes and ships all firing across the screen. More schooldesk letters — AND NOW... OUR FEATURE PRESENTATION. Rosa settled far, far back in her plush red velvet chair. The scenes playing out across her face.

Elvis. Bathing, bare chested in an oval porcelain tub full of steaming sudsy water, his black bullet-studded gun belt slung over the back of the wooden chair next to the tub. Scrubbing his own back with an enormous brush. Cigar in his mouth. He spots a cockroach on the wall, pulls the gun out of its shiny leather holster, cocks and fires. Plaster sprays out of the hole in the wall. A woman runs in from the other room. Julie London in a petticoat. Elvis leaning back, bare chested, into the foamy suds. Laughing now, the cigar between his teeth, the gun smoking in his hand. Julie leans over the tub, hands on her hips, and scolds. "Hey whataya mean shootin' up my hotel like that? What's the big idea?" Elvis grabs her by the arms, leans her farther over the tub and kisses her, hard, on the mouth. Rosa sits far back in her chair. Back in the red velvet. One hand up to her mouth. Fingers on her lips. Elvis in a tub. Rosa in a chair. Julie in a red velvet chair. Rosa in a wooden chair. Elvis with a gun.

waiting for elvis

Julie with a petticoat. Elvis slaps her. Draws a trickle of blood. Julie puts her fingers up to her lips. Pulls them away. When she sees the blood she licks her lips and laughs. Elvis places a cockroach – carefully, lovingly – on her laugh. Elvis with a gun. Rosa in a wooden chair, both of her hands in one of Clothespin Harry's, his other raised, ready. Julie with her cruel hips and petticoats. Julie with her lips. Julie you bitch. Julie you slut. Rosa with a trickle on her lips. Rosa in a petticoat. Elvis. Oh, Elvis.

A convoy of semis thunder by and draw Sal closer, farther from the sanctuary of the forest. He can't help himself now. Starts in counting the wheels on one of the big rigs. Has his own system. Count along one side – not the front tires – multiply by two for the duals, then two again for the other side, then add the front wheels. This rig has two sections so the dollies go two-three-two. A set of two and a set of three on the front trailer, two more on the back, that's seven duals for fourteen count the other side that's another fourteen to make twenty-eight add the front two that's thirty. It's mostly thirty-wheelers he likes to count. Sometimes twenty-six. Not many eighteen anymore. Sal counts them constantly. Can't make himself stop. Spends hours reciting the ritual over and over again as he walks the ditch. He never tires of the math. Never tires of the rhythm of it. Realizes – even as he's doing it – how much he wishes he didn't keep doing it, but he can't help himself. He always says the number out loud when he's done. "Thirty," he says, but not loud enough to hear above the roar. "Twenty-six." The words are lost in the din of a thousand cars and trucks an hour. "Twenty-two." Sal could shout loud enough to hear himself. But he doesn't want to do that. He's not ready.

He will spend the days in the heat and fumes next to the highway, walking through the grey, brittle grass that grows there. The grass gets that way from the constant fallout of gasoline and diesel and oil that settles over the blades day and night. The rain can't keep up – can only wash off a little of the filth – and so the blades get duller and duller, turn brown long before the end of summer. Long before they should. And every spring

waiting for elvis

they come up again, so shiny and green, so new and ready to grow full and rich. But the traffic will already be there, waiting.

Nobody is sightseeing on this stretch of highway. There's nothing to see. Nothing but asphalt and trees and traffic. Unless you count the diner. The one with the faded green sign. The one Sal went over to last night – in spite of himself. Just to see. Never thought he'd end up inside. Sitting down. Let a woman fix him something to eat. It was only that she came out to him. Stepped out into the gathering dusk and took him by the arm. Took him in, the same way his mother used to back home. Except this woman was nothing like Roṣa. Unless it was back when she was still pretty and had a figure. Betty. That was her name.

Cars and trucks hurtle past each other. A cable of speed. A current. Electric. Crackle hum and roar. All day Sal chokes back the exhaust that hangs over the highway, spills over into the forest on either side. The first few feet in, some of the needles on the trees have faded to orange, bark peeling and falling off in flakes. Farther in, where Sal beds down at night, things are a little better. A little greener. A little fresher smelling.

Sal has a place there, thrown together out of scrap wood and metal he picked up out of the ditch or found at the dump he stumbled across just off the highway. The cottagers stop there on their way back to the city and drop off the junk they don't want any longer. Sal can make good use of it. He's found enough material for four walls and a roof, with a table and chairs inside, and a chest of drawers. There's even a television set he found one afternoon, but no electricity for it. A Coleman stove with a kettle and a frying pan. A battered baby blue metal cooler. A lantern for night. Some shelving with a few cans and bottles along one wall. And there's a makeshift sink in one corner with a bucket for water, and in the other corner, an old mattress behind a stack of magazines and newspapers. Sal almost never sleeps there. Most of the time, he spends the night outside, in the hammock he's got strung up between two pine trees farther out in the woods. He feels safer there. There's no

waiting for elvis

door to watch. Like he always did back home. Wait for it to open. Someone to come in.

Still, there is the daily routine of scouring the roadside, the ditch, the space between the trees and the asphalt – forty feet or so – looking for anything that might be of value, of interest. The grass there is cut to six inches or so, just long enough to hide things, things no one notices from the highway. The ditch looks smooth and even from up there. Manicured. Like a lawn. But walk down into it and see how coarse and rough it really is. A long, narrow field of stubble and clumps of sick and dying grass, blades as tough as leather. Walk barefoot over its dusty, uneven surface and your feet will blister and crack, bleed and ache. Your legs will go numb with the effort of keeping your balance. And you will step on things you do not expect, nestled into those six inches of stunted growth.

Today will be like any other day along the highway. Things will come flying off it. Things that got thrown off by the cars and trucks that pass and never stop passing up on the highway. Sal will find them and pick them up. There seems to be something about this particular stretch. A mile or so either side of where the divided ends. A lot of things get thrown out along here. Lost. Discarded. Dislodged. Disconnected. On this stretch it could be almost anything. A window opens and something comes tumbling out. Sal sometimes wonders if they throw things out just for him. If they notice him, walking along the ditch. Toss out some leftover food for him. Half-eaten boxes of Kentucky Fried Chicken. MacDonald's Big Macs. Burger King Whoppers. Crumpled bags of broken cookies, crushed fruit, bruised vegetables, plastic bottles of pop ready to explode, battered cans of beer. And plenty of clothes, too. Once an entire wardrobe, packed neatly into three cardboard boxes, that came flying out of the back of a station wagon. The boxes exploded on impact and spilled their contents as they tumbled through the ditch. Gloves, scarves, sweaters, pants, T-shirts, parkas, bikini tops, panties, slacks. And then there are all the pieces of plastic and metal and glass that come flying off the cars and trucks themselves. Hubcaps, tires, chains, tools, mouldings, mirrors, gas caps. Once, a massive tire, wheel and all, that slipped off a flatbed truck and came bouncing along the shoulder like a crazy giant toy. Sal threw himself out of the way when it rolled down into the ditch and came barrelling right at him, watched it tumble by. It struck a granite boulder at the edge of the woods and bounced high into the air, turned sideways and landed like a donut on the crown of a small spruce tree. Sal got it down with a rope and rolled it back into the woods where he used a length of chain to hoist it into the air with the others. Most of what he finds Sal either buries or stacks in piles – appliances here, bottles there, cans there. If it's something off a car, he takes it to his place in the woods where he's hung them all from ropes and chains. Arranged them so he can swing them back and forth. The last time it was a hot muffler. Scatter bump and roll skidded off the asphalt and down into the ditch. Came to rest at his feet, smoking in the grass, the smell of speed and heat still on it. Then there's all the stuff left after an accident. The bad ones are always along this same stretch. Must be something about four lanes running back into two. Head-on collisions, mostly. Loud enough for Sal to hear even if he's down by the river. Like the distant sound of the steel fist.

Things come flying off the vehicles and end up where no one would think to look. Or care. Sal always waits until the police and ambulance and tow trucks have all gone before he goes to pick anything up. Takes it back with him to hang with the others. Hubcaps. Mufflers. Tires. Bumpers. Roof racks. Windows. Doors. Fenders. Odd pieces of mangled chrome. Car hoods. Truck hoods. Gasoline tanks. Luggage racks. Far too many to count by now – all shapes and sizes – swinging lazily under the tree branches, tinging and binging and gonging against each other in the breeze like some grotesque wind chimes.

Some things he doesn't know what to do with. Like the bag of surgical instruments he found once, scalpels as sharp as razors that cut his skin when he reached into the bag. His thumb bled and bled until he found some bandages in the bag and used them to stop the bleeding. Today, in his sack, Sal's collected a fax machine, a Baby Ruth chocolate bar still in the wrapper, and a box of condoms in a plastic bag with a pair of ladies underwear. The underwear must have been worn already because there were some stain marks at the crotch.

Sometimes the things that come flying out are still alive. Pets. Puppies and kittens, mostly. The tumble doesn't always kill them. He nursed a young pup once, battered and bruised, back to health. Fed it scraps, let it sleep with him in his hammock, strung up between the pines. It ran out into the traffic one morning and became just one more carcass, one more piece of roadkill for Sal to drag off and bury. But it was rolling country there, six lanes each way, not two. And it was ten thousand cars and trucks an hour. So that must have been another highway. Another place. The place where a seven-foot boa rolled across the grass like a log and lay there, stiff and dead he was sure, until just as he reached down to touch it, it suddenly reanimated and slithered away into the woods. So there was nothing to bury. Sal does that with all the animals. Drags them off and gives them a decent burial. Unless the scavengers get to them first. It's a very important thing to do.

It was another place because there was a body there, too – a young woman, her arms and legs broken and mangled, clothes ripped away from her torso, skin torn off one shoulder. Her skull was crushed, nose smashed, teeth shattered. A black mushroom seemed to be growing out of her mouth but it was only her tongue, half bitten off. She hadn't been dead long enough for the smell of decay to set in, but it always comes, and the scavengers with it. They always come for the smell of death.

Sal looked around for a purse that time. A wallet. Some kind of identification. But there was nothing. He thought about dragging her body back up to the edge of the highway and leaving it there on the shoulder, but she'd just as likely get run over by a sleeping trucker if he left her there. So instead he pulled her body up near the pines, dug a hole good and deep at

waiting for elvis

the edge of the woods, and laid her gently into it, covered her with soft red earth and packed it down so the animals wouldn't get to her. Then he went back to his place and made two signs out of cardboard and wooden stakes, wrote a message with a can of black spray paint. He returned to where he'd buried her and waited until dark before he ran up to the road and hammered a sign that read "WOMAN DEAD" into the dirt with his spade. A black arrow pointed to the woods. He pounded the other sign in at the foot of her grave. It said, "HER" with an arrow pointing at the ground. After that he slipped into the forest and made for home. Stayed there for three days because he didn't want to be around when they came for her. Didn't want any questions. Questions about who he was and what he was doing there. Something like that could bring the steel fist thundering down in broad daylight out of the blue sky. When he finally did go he saw the grave had been opened and the body removed. Sal found some yellow police tape still stuck in the branch of a tree and knew it must have been the cops. They even took away the signs. So then they wouldn't come snooping around. Just the same, Sal moved on after that. Best to. Just be left alone. That was best.

Just at dusk Sal is on his way home, hugging the treeline, lights coming on in cars and trucks all up and down the highway like a river of stars twinkling into existence, when he spots a fox pulling at something on the ground. Tugging at something half buried there. They come out at dusk, the scavengers. Too much daylight doesn't suit them. Sal's heart pumps faster. His hands clam over instantly as he opens and closes them, opens and closes them. Then his mouth. Open and closed. Open and closed. Sal is having trouble breathing. He can't get any air. Most of the time he just leaves the animals to themselves and they do the same for him, but not when he sees them doing something like this. Trying to get at something in the ground. That can bring the steel fist quick and terrible swooping down out of the indigo sky. Sal tries to wave off the fox, who looks up at him, bares its teeth. Sal knows this animal.

waiting for elvis

Knows the white marks on her front legs. She comes around his place sometimes, always after him for any scrap of food. Anything for her pups. He tosses her a little something and shoos her off. Throws a boot at her when she won't leave. Sal hears himself yell out at the fox now and kicks out a heel at her. She shows him her fangs and snarls. He kicks at her again and she moves off. Knows enough to stay out of reach of his boot. Moves off to a safe distance and watches as Sal bends low to get a better look.

Sal straightens up after he's made sure that what she's been tugging at is not a baby's arm. No. Just a flattened racoon carcass. So then Sal won't have to scrape away the dry dirt and lift out a box, a cardboard box, flaps folded over neatly, tucked into each other, a white box that says "OREOS" on both sides in big blue letters. Lift it out and open it up to see that it isn't a baby, still alive, squirming, arms up and hands fisted into the air. No. No. Just a racoon.

So it's okay to head back into the trees. They always take him back in, the trees. Just like Rosa did back home. Never turn him away. Not even after that first steel fist hit him full force, crashed him into a violent stupor that left him paralyzed. Frozen. Shattered. Even then his mother took him into her arms. Held him. Protected him as best she could. Gave him rest. Rosa, quiet. Waiting for it to pass. Until it did, embrace him. Still. Enfold him, the way the trees do every night after he's climbed up into his hammock where the night creatures won't bother him. Give him relief. Give him rest.

Where is home? He wonders. Just how far has he come from the place he and his mother lived for all those years? Remembers something now. Suddenly. Completely. That's the way things come back to him. The same way they come flying out of the cars and trucks that hurtle by. No warning. Out of nowhere. No time to get out of the way. No way to run. To hide.

Clothespin Harry thrashing violently out of his sleep – as if thrown from a train, eyes wide and terrible as murder – just at the moment they come in through the door. Sal frozen with the keys to the pickup in his hand, dangling like a pendulum, just as he's about to put them back on the kitchen table. Harry figuring out everything in an instant. Fury that spins him up off the couch to grab Sal by the throat, as if he might pick him up and throw him through the window. But then he turns calm. A calm that is worse than anything that came before it. That's when Sal knows something bad is coming. He wants to turn and run, screaming, from the room, but he's too frightened.

"I'll have to hurt you now, Big Son," says Harry. "For what you did." He looks up at Rosa. "I'll take care of you later. Besides," and a big smile starts up on his face, "you get to watch." He undoes the button on Sal's pants, slowly, deliberately, and pulls them down gently. "Just remember, now. I don't want you to make a sound. You know how important that is, don't you, Big Son." He sits Sal, naked now from the waist down, up on the edge of the wooden chair, so that Sal's testicles – still hairless organs he has not yet paid much attention to – hang over the edge of the chair, between his pale legs. "It's going to sneak up on you, this hurt," says Harry, and takes a clothespin down off his helmet, examines it, fondles it for a few seconds before placing it – delicately, surgically – on Sal's right testicle. "Sneak up and just eat you up, that's what this hurt will do. But hold it in now, Big Son. Hold it in. Make your mother proud." Harry takes down another pin and positions it on Sal's other testicle.

And it's true, what Harry says. At first it doesn't really hurt very much at all. Clothespin Harry just sits there watching. Waiting. Looking into Sal's eyes, smiling. And when he sees in them the hurt starting up, out of a faraway place – like a punch coming out of the darkness – his smile gets bigger and bigger as the pain increases. Even Sal smiles a little, at first. Smiles back at Harry. He doesn't know what else to do. He doesn't know how to do anything but let himself go. Into the pain. Just before he does he looks over at his mother, crying, shoulders shaking. She's never seen me in this kind of pain before, thinks Sal. He loves her even more, then, when he sees her tears – feels a deep sense of joy mixed in with the deep, frightening hollow purple pain growing stronger and stronger in his testicles. Rosa loves me, he thinks. She does.

The pain rolls higher and deeper, until finally Sal just lets go and passes out. When he comes to, the pins are back on Harry's hat. "I told you it would sneak up on you, didn't I? Was I right? You see what I mean? You can take my word on that. Every time. That's something isn't it? Some kind of pain. Nothing like it on earth. A thing of beauty." Later, his mother with a bowl of ice water cupped in her hands, setting it down on the floor for Sal to squat into so his purple and swollen sack can hang down into it. Her squatting next to him. The two of them like that, for a long time.

Sal's mother used to tell about how Elvis – the real Elvis Presley – had a little twin brother that nobody knew about. Sal never liked that story much. It scared him every time he heard it, but his mother used to love telling it and so he always listened.

"The doctor saw that something else was getting born along with Elvis," said his mother, "but instead of another healthy pink baby what came out was something else. Something awful. Nothing like a baby at all. More like a ball of hair and bone and skin, legs and face and hands all rolled up inside it. At first they weren't sure what it was, didn't know what to think, but then they got it all untangled and there it was. A hairy little creature. Tiny little claws on the ends of his fingers. A boy. Elvis' little twin brother. Born dead, some say. Some say not."

His mother told that story sometimes after they finished listening to Elvis sing on the old turntable that used to sit in the corner of the kitchen, next to the window, before Harry kicked it into kindling and wire. It was Sal who always used to put the needle down on the record, the record that was always there, waiting to be played.

"Could you play that song for me again, Salazar?" his mother would say.

"Which song is that?" Sal would ask, even though he knew perfectly well.

"You know the one." His mother would be sitting in her old wicker chair out on the porch, Sal at her feet, head leaned into her lap.

waiting for elvis

"Sure," he'd say, and get up and go in through the screen door and put the needle down gently so by the time he got back out to the porch Elvis was already singing "Are You Lonesome Tonight?" while his mother leaned back in her wicker chair and stroked Sal's head with her shiny warm palm and said, "Thank you, Salazar. I do love it so." Sometimes, instead of going back in to pick up the needle after the song was over, Sal would let the record spin while they listened to it skip over and over again in the same place, a companion to their even, rhythmic breathing.

Sometimes his mother would take one of his hands in hers and say, "These, you got from your dad. You have your father's hands. Just like they were carved out of stone. A few more years and they'll be just like his. Like two pieces of marble."

Not like Clothespin Harry's hands. Small. Girlish. Delicate. Sal, in spite of himself, sometimes found himself inspecting Harry's hands carefully, even as they performed their work with such surgical precision.

"Not cold or hard to the touch, mind you," his mother would say, "but soft. And warm. Like the sun. He'd pick you up and cradle you in the palm of his hand. Hold you up in front of him like you were a cloud he could blow away. He'd pick me up too, sometimes, naked out of the bathtub in one swoop, like I was a bird. I weighed almost nothing back then, mind you. Scoop me up out of the bath, carry me over to the bed, lay me on the covers, dry me like I was a flower with those big hands of his. I was still pretty then. I still had a figure." His mother only ever talked about Sal's father when Harry wasn't around.

"Or he'd come up behind me at the kitchen sink, put his hands on my waist and spin me around. Pull me up close to him. I was just this little wisp back then. Not much more than a schoolgirl. The feeling of that. Him pulling me close like that. Leaning over me, close, kissing me on my mouth. That was the best time, Salazar. The best time of all. And you. You came from that time. From that place."

Her features darkened. Her eyes lost their shine. "And look at us now. Look what's happened to us. There's just Harry for us now." Sal knew if his father ever came back Clothespin Harry would be dead. Dead and buried. And all this would be just like a dream they woke up from. A nightmare. Harry and his clothespins and his little girl hands. And his mother trying to please him just so they could eat and she could have her bottle, the one she was pouring out of now, into that same chipped teacup she always drank out of. Drank without enjoyment while she rubbed a smoke-stained hand – fingers swollen from clutching at Harry's pain – a hand that smelled acrid and sickly sweet from the cigarettes and liquor, against Sal's cheek.

"What happened to him?" Sal would sometimes ask, before she drifted too far away.

"What's that, Salazar?"

"To my father. What happened to him?"

"He left."

"But why?"

"Same reason as any man."

"What's that?"

"Why, no reason at all, Salazar. No reason at all."

"That doesn't make sense."

"A man doesn't need a reason. He just gets up one morning and you look into his face and you see something's gone. You see it missing from his eyes. Or maybe his mouth. The way he moves his lips while he's eating his eggs. The way he puts on his boots. You see it. And you know right there nothing can ever be the same again. The next thing you see is him walking away, out the door and through the pines. And you never see him again."

Sal has a picture in his mind of his father's back – not like Harry's back at all. Not curved like a reptile and sneaky strong mean, but straight and wide and walking away between the trees. It's always sunny and early in the day. Morning sounds crackle and snap under his father's boots and the frost clouds up his breath. He never turns around. Never waves. So Sal never gets to see his face. Just those big hands swinging at his sides, that broad back walking away.

A quick sharp flash of something through a crack in the traffic brings Sal up onto the shoulder. The bustle of heat and fumes are like a hot liquid wave that pushes away the cooler evening air. Something in the median, in the grassy hollow between the east- and westbound lanes. A creature of some kind, visible only in snatches, when his line of vision allows for a clear view across all six lanes. It's always hard to make things out there. Easy to think you imagined it. Something small, about the size of a racoon or a fox, but the fur is too thick, too dark. Not a badger or a lynx. The head is too big. A bear cub, maybe. A longer break in the traffic allows him to see the hunched back of a small apelike creature squatting in the dirty grass. It turns to look over its shoulder at him. A face with lips and white teeth and eyes under a sloping forehead. Hands for paws. Fingers. A small human-looking creature, covered in hair. A baby. But not a baby. Moving now along the median. Back and forth on short stumpy legs. Crawling. One way. Then the other. Looking at Sal the whole time. Searching. Searching for a way over. Something familiar in the slope of the shoulders. In the way the hair at the back of the neck stands up.

The traffic creates a strobe effect now – each frame a flash of the creature's movements – a split-second tableau. A sinewy arm poised under the torso. A small red mouth. Open. Closed. Open. White teeth. Body coming out of a crouch. Straightening up. Standing now. Awkwardly. As though for the first time in its young life. It's him alright, thinks Sal. So he did get born. Somehow I always knew this day would come. I should have known he'd be the one to find me. The creature raises one arm now to point a finger at him. At Sal. Then a convoy of big rigs cuts him off completely and after they pass he's gone. Vanished. But it's true. He's here.

chapter three

It's a cold, drizzly day with a fine mist that hovers thickly over the grass and concrete corridor cut through the Canadian Shield. Arty has the wipers on intermittent as they drive to the diner and Betty, drifting in and out of sleep, looks out the window at the spruce trees slipping by like so many days of her life. So green. Every needle dripping moisture. Someone out in the open, next to the trees, bent low over the stubble, long coat stretched across his wide wet back, shoulders sloped. Pulling at something there. In the dirty grass. Something that might be a leg. Or maybe an arm. Betty has a sudden and powerful image of her father, hunched over the dead German soldier. He's just taken the soldier's heavy overcoat from him, put it on himself, and now he's checking the pockets for anything else that might be of some value or interest.

The wipers kick in again and Betty is Elizabeth, a little girl of six, just up out of her bed and walking across the cold hardwood of the hallway toward the kitchen. There's some kind of commotion there. The unfamiliar baritone of a man's voice. She stops in the doorway. A strange man in a uniform is standing at the kitchen table, talking to her mother.

"Look at this," he says, lifting an enormous metal tray out of the huge olive green duffle bag on the floor in front of him. He

waiting for elvis

hands it to Betty's mother. She takes it in her two hands, holds it out in front of her awkwardly.

"It's heavy," she says, and puts it down on the kitchen table.

"It should be," says the man. "It's made of solid silver."

He bends down and pulls a great grey coat out of the bag. "And how about this?"

"What did you want to bring that back for?"

"Took it off a Kraut," he says.

"It's filthy," says her mother.

"Souvenir. Anyway, the Kraut sure as hell didn't need it anymore." He laughs, and just then Betty steps into the room.

"Elizabeth," says her mother. "Look who it is. Your father's come home."

"Hello, Lizzie," says the man. He smiles down at her.

"Say hello to your father," says Betty's mother. There are little tight lines around her mouth and eyes.

Betty hasn't seen her father in four years – doesn't really remember much about him. Just sometimes before she goes to sleep a face close to hers and a pair of big warm hands and the sound of a low voice. She's come to think of that man as nothing more than an image in the pictures her mother keeps on the mantel and up in her bedroom. And now here he is, standing in the brightly lit kitchen with that enormous heavy coat in his hands.

"Remember me?" Her father drapes the coat across the table and looks down at her.

"Hello, Daddy," says Betty.

"Go on," says Betty's mother and motions Betty closer.

Her father sits down on one of the steel-framed chairs. Betty walks over and lets herself be lifted up and placed on his knee. Her father puts one arm around her and brings his face up next to hers so that she can feel the sting of the prickly stubble on his cheek. He picks up a bottle of beer from the table and takes a long drink.

Betty's mother picks up the coat and holds it out in front of her, turns it one way, then another. "What's this?" she says, and pokes a finger through a hole in the fabric.

"What does it look like?" says Betty's father.

"Good heavens, George."

Another swipe of the wipers and the coat is folded neatly in Betty's two hands, cleaned and washed and just lifted out of her mother's old trunk. She and Arty were moving her into a small apartment and going through some of her things and there it was. Betty's father was long gone by then but her mother had kept the coat in that trunk all those years. She put it in with all the other clothes she wanted to throw out, but Arty spotted it and rescued it from the pile, recognized it instantly for what it was and started in about how he was going to hang it up on the coat rack at the diner.

"Truckers'll get a kick out of it," he said. "You'll see."

"They'll think it's just some smelly old coat somebody left behind," said Betty.

"It's got a whole story behind it."

"But they won't know that."

"That's the beauty. They will after I tell them."

"Oh, I see. They get the story from you, do they?"

"A real conversation piece. That's what this is."

So now the coat has been hanging there, on the coat rack next to the door, for as long as anyone can remember. Once in a while Arty still tells the story and one of the truckers will take it off the rack and try it on, or maybe just poke his finger through the bullet hole. That's mostly what they seem to want to do. Follow the path of that imaginary bullet.

Betty sits up in the car, turns her head to look back along the treeline. Wonders if it was him. The man who came into the diner a few days back wearing a long coat of his own – pockets stuffed to bursting.

"What is it?" says Arty.

"Nothing," says Betty. "Thought I saw something, that's all."

"Deer like to come out and graze in this weather. Bound to be a few killed on this stretch today."

Arty's right. Hardly a day goes by in the summer they don't spot one dead at the side of the road, crows and magpies already feasting. Sometimes a loaded semi hits one so hard it leaves a bright splash of blood on the concrete highway like a can of red paint exploded. That's probably the best way, thinks Betty. Better than getting their back legs smashed before they drag themselves into the ditch to die a slow, painful death. She's seen that, too.

For the rest of the morning Betty finds herself thinking about the coat. Her father. The stranger. Every time she walks by the coat rack with a coffee pot or a tray of cinnamon buns, it strikes her as funny that she should have imagined it was her father bent over like that. Wearing the coat. She never did see him with it on. And what about the stranger? Maybe it was the coat that brought him into the diner that night. Maybe he spotted it hanging there next to the door and thought he might like to have it. Maybe that was what made him leave the cover of the woods to cross the open parking lot.

But then Harvey pulls into the parking lot, only this time instead of just him getting off, the whole bus empties out into the diner and the place turns into chaos. One minute it's quiet, a few truckers nursing their coffee and making small talk with Arty, and the next, thirty silver-haired women clutching sweaters and purses are clambering off Harvey's Greyhound air-conditioned bus. Every time Betty comes back to the counter for something, Harvey beams at her like a puppy waiting to be patted. He's been talking to Arty through the serving window. Betty's got Arty back there cutting up buns and setting them out on plates for her to take over to the booths while he listens to Harvey explain how the traffic wasn't too bad and by the time he got up to the diner he was ahead of schedule and decided at the last minute to turn in and give those old ladies a taste of Betty's famous giant cinnamon buns. How he worked them into a froth about how good they are. Made it sound like this is a once-in-a-lifetime chance.

"Thought you could use the business," he says when Betty goes by with the coffee. "I figure it's the least I can do. What with you having all these men in here all the time, belching and swearing and smelling up the place. A busload of sweet-smelling old ladies is just the ticket." Harvey holds his cup out to Betty. "Say, could you top me up while you're at it? Thanks." He stares into the cleavage between the folds of her white blouse while she pours. She's used to that by now. Men doing that. Betty dresses comfortable – blue jeans and a loose-fitting white cotton shirt with a couple of buttons open at the top. That's her outfit. It's cool and comfortable and she feels good wearing it. Arty brought her a couple of uniforms to try once – the kind the waitresses wear in the city – but Betty couldn't stand the way they made her feel – like she was working for someone else.

"This is my place," she said to Arty when he gave her a hard time about it. "Mine as much as it is yours. I don't need to walk around here looking like I'm the hired help, because I'm not." She stuffed the uniforms into a box up on one of the shelves in back, in case they ever have to hire anybody, and maybe whoever the girl is can make use of them. Until then, that's where they're staying.

Harvey's no different than any of the other men who come into the place. Big men mostly, with company logos for Reimer and Arnold Brothers and Paul's Hauling on their soiled baseball caps. Their stomachs hang over their brass belt buckles, which are always in the shape of a rig or a naked woman or a cowboy. When they walk in they push their caps up on their shiny foreheads and slap each other on the back. Sit down in one of the Formica booths and wave Betty over to pour them some coffee. Maybe ask for a cinnamon bun. When she brings it over they look her up and down. Make no secret about it. The ones with a little imagination try to flirt with her. Try to make her laugh. Sometimes there might be one of them with wide shoulders and a slim waist and a sense of what a woman wants to hear. Those are the dangerous ones. But she always makes sure they know where the line is.

She can't stop the talk, though. The things they say when they don't think she or Arty can hear.

"That's some ass on her, eh?"

"Built for speed."

"Tits aren't bad either."

"Bet she could make a guy go off soft."

They talk like that sometimes. Arty hears it, too. Gets fed up.

"If that peckerhead says one more thing I'm going over there and drop him," he'll say to Betty at the counter.

"No you won't," says Betty.

"A guy can only take so much. At least from a smelly son of a bitch like him." It might be one of truckers with a load of squealing hogs sitting out in the parking lot. There are more and more of them these days and they bring the stink right in with them. "If he makes one more crack about your tits."

"And my ass," says Betty. "Don't forget about my ass."

"Jesus, Betty."

"Forget him."

"Maybe if you didn't give him so much to look at." Arty indicates the modest bit of cleavage at the top of her white blouse.

"Christ, Arty, you're not going to start this again."

"Start what?"

Betty could throw it all back in his face anytime she wants to but she never does. When they first started up, it was Arty always hinting she could stand to undo a button or two on her blouse, let them see a little more of her.

"You want me to show them my tits," she said the first time he did it. "Is that what you want?"

"Christ no, Betty. All I'm saying is you could jazz up your outfit a little, that's all."

"I'm nothing fancy, Arty. I never will be."

"That's the beauty, Betty. Some women are all sizzle and no steak, but not you. You're the straight goods. Meat and potatoes. Just what a trucker wants. But just a little sizzle wouldn't hurt. That's all I'm saying."

"You sure you know what you're asking for?"

Next morning, before she went to serve the first pair of truckers, Betty undid a couple of buttons so the first naked curves of her breasts showed between the folds of her blouse.

waiting for elvis

She could feel the air there – cool against her naked breastbone – when she walked out from behind the counter, a little blush washing down into her blouse with it. It was a long walk over to the booth where she poured coffee into the cups of the men and felt them look at her while they made small talk the same as they always did. There was nothing much different about it until she turned to walk back to the counter. That was when she felt it – the crackle in the air that hadn't been there before. It was them looking after her, then looking at each other. She'd never been the kind of woman to try and get attention from men that way, and she'd never thought she'd like the taste of it, but there it was: a little spicy, a little bitter at the back of her throat. She didn't like the way it made her feel, and yet, she kind of liked the way it made her feel. It was like that for the rest of the day. And the next. Meanwhile, the buttons stayed undone while she tried to figure out how to feel about the way she felt. That was years ago and she still hasn't worked her way through it. All she knows is she's proud to have kept her figure. And she likes the idea that she could still turn a man's head if she wanted to. Still, Arty's got nothing to fear. Betty isn't looking. And if she was, she sure as hell wouldn't be looking in a place like this.

Arty puts another tray of cinnamon buns up on the service counter. There's sweat running down both of his temples and he's breathing heavily. "I hope you don't mind my saying," he says to Harvey through the window, "but is there any way you could give us a heads-up next time?"

"I don't see how," says Harvey.

"I don't suppose."

"I just thought you could use the business, is all."

"And we appreciate it, Harvey. Don't think we don't appreciate it."

"I can just as easy drive these old broads right on by from now on."

"Look. I didn't mean anything, okay? Forget what I said."

"Pretty soon it won't matter one way or the other, I guess."

"What does that mean?"

"You said yourself the place probably won't be here much longer. Not if the divided comes through. Surveyors are out again today."

"I know. I saw them, too. It's not them I'm worried about, Harvey. It's the guys in suits carrying briefcases. That's when the trouble starts."

"I'd hold out. Make 'em pay."

"Market value. That's all they have to give me. I checked on it."

"Might be more than you think."

"For Chrissake there's nothing around here for miles and miles but bush and rock, Harvey. And let's face it. The place isn't exactly in mint condition."

"They gotta make you a decent offer."

"It won't be enough."

"Well, they can't just come in here and start bulldozing the place down. I know that much. We got laws."

Betty hears the two of them going at it but she doesn't have time to pay much attention. Besides. Talk like that all sounds the same. And this busload of women is putting her to the test. A lot of them want tea. That means a cup and saucer, a tea bag and hot water in a separate pot. The whole ritual. She had to get Arty to dig out some more stainless steel pots from one of the back cupboards and bring down the extra china cups and saucers she had stored in the back. She made him wash and dry them before he set them out on the service window for her to take to the booths. She never has to work this hard for a room full of men. Coffee's so much easier. You put the cup down and fill it. Betty's thinking how maybe a room full of cap-wearing, beer-bellied truck drivers has something to be said for it. In the time it's taken her to get these ladies their buns and beverages two shifts of truckers could have come and gone.

She hands Arty a bun through the window.

"Toast that one," she says.

"What the hell?" Betty's giant cinnamon buns are not the kind you toast. They're too big, and dripping with syrup.

"Use the oven if you have to. I don't know. Oh, and hold the butter. She doesn't want any butter."

"Christ."

The ladies wait patiently, purses in their laps, white hair perfect, while Betty sets out the cups and saucers – some still warm from Arty washing them. As she serves them she picks up bits of their conversation. It all sounds the same from one booth to the next. The kind of talk that's interchangeable. That makes no more sense than the predictable exchange Arty and Harvey are having. Instead of tobacco and aftershave lotion these ladies give off the scent of cheap perfume and medication. Some of them are busy making a tremendous fuss over Betty's cinnamon buns. Taking large forkfuls into their cavernous mouths, mashing them around with false teeth and coated tongues. Bits of bun travel to the edges of their mouths. Stay there. A small droplet of cinnamon syrup on the chin of one lady. A tea stain on the blouse of another.

Betty finds herself looking at their hands, boney and fleshless, as they cradle their teacups. Skin translucent. Veins blue and shiny. They bring the cups up to their lips with the fingertips of both hands. The lips, wrinkled and dry, are covered over with a thick layer of blood-red lipstick that sticks to the edge of the cup, leaves a garish red mark there that will have to be scrubbed away. She wonders how they ended up here, these women. Like this. On a bus tour, heading for the city to gamble their pensions away. That's the run Harvey's on. He takes a load in every week from places like Kenora and Dryden, Fort Francis and Atikokan. Sometimes it's a day trip. Sometimes it's overnight. The big casinos have hotels built onto them so women like this never have to leave the building if they don't want to. Most of them are widows, Betty guesses. They've lost their husbands to heart attack and stroke and cancer and alcoholism. And now the kids have put them into a seniors home and they don't see much of them because it's a long drive out from the city. There are too many days with nothing to do but sit in the room and wait for the next meal. Maybe watch a little television in the lounge. Go to the bathroom. So when there's a chance to head into the city for a day of gambling at the casino, why not? All they have to do is get on the bus. The rest is all taken care of.

They've embraced their old age, these women. It shows in the way they conduct themselves – with a certain sense of entitlement. They seem almost eager to indulge in eccentricity. Disapproval and impatience lie just beneath their insular conversation. It shows through in the way they compliment Betty on her cinnamon buns with one breath, then complain about a bent fork, a missing napkin, a hairline crack in a saucer with the next. In much of what they say and do there is the contingency for annoyance, displeasure, inconvenience. It's all they have left. The last few vestiges of power to wield over the small, tightly-wound circle of their decline.

Betty wonders whether her own mother might have ended up this way – if things had turned out differently. She tries to imagine her sitting at one of the booths. Settled in with a group of these women, making this kind of conversation. The reality of her mother's existence is a one-room apartment – one she shares with her constant companion. Betty's mother is never alone. Not a day, not an hour goes by, that her mother hasn't committed to a long-term relationship she began soon after Betty's father died. Ever since that day – week after week, year after year – her mother has remained faithful, her fidelity unshakeable. Never once has she strayed from the sacred covenant of her alcoholic ritual.

Betty will have to go and visit soon. She won't be able to last much longer before the guilt gets to her and breaks her down, like it always does eventually. Then she'll get in the truck and drive into the city. Her mother's place is on the second floor of an old brick block off West Broadway. The place is crawling with boozers and beggars and schizophrenics. Betty's mother does not bother to concern herself with any of these people. She has her liquor and a few groceries delivered regularly and never leaves the apartment. The squalor of her daily existence rivals anything the dealers and crack whores and drinkers that live in the other rooms can muster. Every once in a while somebody breaks in and steals the booze out of her room while she's passed out. Betty's mother orders more. A young crackhead broke in and tried to rape her once but she grabbed a bottle of Lamb's and hit him over the head with it. Then she pulled down her skirt and dropped the big orange onyx ashtray from the coffee table on his head a couple of times for good measure. Now she has a reputation. They leave her alone.

Betty's mother uses lipstick, too. Paints on a thick layer several times a day just like these women do. Leaves ugly marks on all the glasses strewn around the apartment. But her mother has aged in a different way. The drinking and smoking have turned her skin the colour of clay, cracked her cheeks into dried mud, cut deep lines across her forehead. The cigarettes have stained her fingers brown and yellowed her teeth. There are layers and folds in the bags under her ravaged eyes, their deep blue long ago clouded over with a curtain of smoke and ash. Her cough comes as thick and liquid as the black tar in her lungs, and the stink of her is thicker.

The drinking starts first thing in the morning with a glass of Lamb's, cut with a little bit of Coca Cola flat and warm out of the can that sits open on the beside table overnight. Not too much early in the day. Just enough to get things back on an even keel. Save the heavy going for later in the day. That's when the serious drinking begins. Set a good rhythm and keep it steady. Later, pass out in front of the television. Get up and make it to the bed if she can. Either way, start up again the next morning.

Betty's taking a bit of a break now, sitting on a stool behind the counter, watching as the ladies sip their tea noisily, four and five to a booth, chewing down their cinnamon buns. Is this the way she'll end up? After Arty's gone – dead of a heart attack, most likely. He has the build for it. The personality. The way he insists on hanging on to his anger, his diet of greasy food, both of them stored up in that stomach of his, the one he got from all those years of trucking. Will she make the same pact these

waiting for elvis

women have made? The one that makes it necessary to keep so much hidden? How many secrets, Betty wonders, will they take with them to their waiting graves? That only they know. About their children. Their husbands. Themselves. All the peaks and valleys of their sacrifice, their longing. Betty watches them as they sit in the comfort of their carefully crafted conversation. So insulated from each other. From themselves. Is that what she has to look forward to?

As if on a signal the women begin to open up their enormous purses and dig into them. Bottles and vials appear on the tables. They open them with great care, take out pills and tablets and patches, and begin the careful ingestion of their daily medication. Almost all of them are taking something – many two or three or four different medications. Betty can guess what they're for. Blood pressure, heart murmur, blood clot, glaucoma, diabetes, cholesterol, arthritis, rheumatism, constipation, diarrhoea. She knows the list. A lot of them must have the same conditions her mother drowns in alcohol.

Harvey leaves her a five-dollar tip at the counter and goes to use the bathroom before he starts herding the women back onto the bus. They're still filing out the door when a couple of motorcycles pull up noisily out front. Through the dusty windowpanes Betty can make out Tony and some of the others from town. They dismount like cowboys and walk across the gravel toward the door. When they get inside they stand at the entrance in their black leather jackets and chains, a cigarette dangling from Tony's lips as he sneers at the old women who have lifted their heads to stare. He walks over to the counter like he's entitled to all of it – but wants none of it – same as he does every place Betty's ever seen him walk into. He's always had that about him. That attitude.

The others follow him over to the counter and sit down on stools. There are three of them with Tony – a woman and two men. Betty's knows who they are. She's seen them around town. They're exactly the reason she didn't want Tony getting the bike in the first place. The woman's name is Grace. She's older than these boys. Older looking, too. There's nothing young and pretty about her. She is hard and rough and even in the curves of her hips under her tight black leather pants there's nothing soft. Her thick lips look freshly swollen, as though from sex or violence, and she has a mouth full of enormous crooked teeth. She has short messy blond hair, earrings that dangle over her shoulders, and a t-shirt under her jacket that reads "Dirty Girl." There is a deep, asymmetrical line of cleavage there, just above the letters.

The two men are also familiar to Betty. One of them is tall with a neatly trimmed beard, the other shorter and stockier with a long ponytail hanging down the back of his battered jacket.

"Joint's jumpin'," says Tony.

"Fuck me sideways," says the man with the ponytail. His name is Eddy. He's looking around at the old women, who are trying not to be too obvious in their stares.

"Night of the living dead," says Carl. Betty remembers their names from when they came to help Tony fix the bike. She's standing in front of them now, on the other side of the counter, coffee pot in one hand, a cup in the other.

"That for me?" says Grace. "I could sure use it." She stares up at Betty. Chews and smacks her gum noisily. Grins with a mouth full of yellow teeth.

"So what's good," says Carl, smiling through his neatly trimmed beard.

Tony looks over at them. "We don't have time to eat. Remember?"

"What do you want?" says Betty matter-of-factly. She looks only at Tony.

"Pa around?" he says.

"He's out back." Betty can guess what they came for. Tony's going to ask Arty for money. That's the only thing that ever brings him around. The only time he'll let himself be seen in the place. But he knows better than to ask her for it.

"Hey Tony," says Grace. "Is your old lady always this friendly?" She smiles up at Betty, but behind the smile there is defiance.

Betty turns back slowly to look at her. Grips the handle of the coffee pot tighter. Lowers the cup slowly down onto the counter.

"Fuck me tenderly," says Eddy, still looking around at all the women. "Is it always like this in here?"

"It's a granny convention," says Carl. "Never seen so many smelly old broads in one room."

"You can go through there," Betty says to Tony, and tilts her head to indicate the back entrance.

"I'll be right back," says Tony.

"Take your friends with you," says Betty evenly.

"I guess we better go, fellas," says Grace. "We wouldn't want to get on the wrong side of an old boot."

The coffee pot is trembling in Betty's hand. She uses the other hand to steady it.

"I didn't mean you," says Grace. "Did you think I meant you?"

When Betty doesn't answer Tony gets up off the stool and waves them in behind him. "Come on," he says. "Let's get the fuck out of here."

"See ya, Betty," says Grace. "It is Betty, isn't it?" She gets up and follows Tony through to the back, but her eyes stay on Betty until she's through the doorway.

Betty lowers the coffee pot. Sets it down slowly. Steadies herself against the counter. Unclenches her jaw.

Later, headed back to town, she finds herself inspecting the treeline on either side of the highway while Arty drives. He could be a thousand miles away by now, the stranger. Or dead. Or standing just inside the cover of the darkening woods, watching them go by. She and Arty never do much talking on the drive home unless it's something to do with the diner. Or maybe Tony. Either way it never takes more than a minute or two to get it said. Then it's back to silence. Betty's thinking about what she'd do if she did spot him – the stranger. Sal. If that's his name. If she didn't imagine the letters of it there in the swirls of the cinnamon syrup. She doesn't think she's ever heard

waiting for elvis

that name before and yet it's somehow familiar. She'd have to make Arty stop the car. Get out and go down into the ditch to talk to him. Call him by that name. To see his reaction. Tell him it's alright to come around to the diner. No matter what Arty said.

But they're coming out of the Shield now – forest giving way to open fields and prairie sky – and there's been no sign of him. Hayden is in sight now, the first few lights of town shimmering in the dusk. Home, thinks Betty. I'm on my way home. And yet, it doesn't feel anything like that. Hasn't for some time now.

chapter four

SAL, OUT IN THE OPEN, CAUGHT BETWEEN THE HIGHWAY and the trees. Inching closer. In spite of himself. He's learned not to get too close to the traffic. Like the time he was walking along the edge of the asphalt and a Bic lighter caught him on the shoulder. It left an ugly black bruise that refused to go away for weeks. Even something that small can do a lot of damage when it comes flying out of a car. Still, it's nothing like the steel fist. Nothing at all.

Moving closer now. Closer to the traffic. Sal wants to see for himself whether Little Elvis might still be there. In the median. Like he was last time. Sal could never survive there. Not with all that traffic. Not even fit for an animal there. Getting caught between the lanes will finish you for sure. Crash your senses. Shotgun blast and black pounding punch to the head. Fever. Sal has seen what it can do. He saw a doe get caught in there once, between the lanes of heavy summer traffic. It stumbled and staggered around in there, confused and terrified by the chaos of the noise – the scream of tires and roar of engines, the fumes and the heat – until the madness of all those cars and trucks made it buck and kick, snarl and swirl and spin out of control, then make a tremendous leap that almost cleared two lanes of traffic,

waiting for elvis

but a black Lincoln Navigator going far too fast clipped the hindquarters with a knuckle crunch and thump that sent it sprawling into the ditch while Sal watched. The doe raised herself up on her front legs, hooves punched into the grass, and she started for the trees, dragging her hindquarters – legs smashed, bone sticking out through the skin – across the filthy stubble. Left a trail of blood and bits of flesh and hide.

Sal followed her, surprised by how quickly she moved, how fast she had pulled herself into the cover of the forest. He saw where she disappeared into the trees and entered carefully. He didn't want to frighten her into running any farther than she had to. Not like that. Then he saw her, lying exhausted, panting heavily through pink, foaming nostrils, under the cover of a low-hanging spruce bough. Her head was still up, brown eyes wide, full of pain and terror. Slowly, tenderly, Sal knelt next to her. Reached out one great hand and ran it warm along the top of her head. Spoke to her gently as he stroked the hot, silky smoothness of her fur.

"Shhh," he said. "Shhh. It hurts. I know. It hurts. But I'm gonna fix it. Fix it so it won't hurt anymore." And as he knelt he reached very carefully into the big outside pocket of his coat and pulled out the little black spade he always carried with him – the one that folds up small enough for him to tuck away there. Unfolded it, never taking his eyes off the doe. Gripped it tightly with both hands.

"Okay," he said to her. She looked up at him with her wet brown eyes, tears thick as tree sap along the bridge of her nose. Sal lifted the spade high. Kept it there, poised above her head because she'd turned to look for a moment into the trees. Deep into the darkness there. And Sal wanted to let her do that. Look once more into the forest she'd known all her life. Take one last look at the place she loved. And when she turned back to Sal, and looked up at him, she had the same look his mother used to get when Clothespin Harry was getting ready to hurt her. When her eyes would tell him there was nothing else to do but give in. Give in to the pain.

waiting for elvis

"Okay?" said Sal again. And this time the answer was in her eyes and Sal brought the edge of the spade down hard and split her skull open with such force that bits of red and pink and grey splattered across his hands and face. Her legs stiffened strangely, straightened out in a long, long stretch – the back arched in a slow languid curve of her spine. Her eyes clouded over, and her tongue fell, long and pale, out of her open mouth. Sal watched her blood seep thick and black into the needles of the forest floor. There was a moment of stillness between them. Of peace. When all the traffic sounds disappeared while he listened to the small sounds of her dying. A last tiny gurgle of blood. A barely audible moan. It was always like that with animals in the forest. The way life left them. With such small sweet steps.

Sal used the spade to dig a shallow grave and pulled her into it, covered her over with moist dirt and leaves and bits of twig. It was never any trouble, doing that. Giving them a decent burial. Then he folded up the spade and tucked it into the large side pocket of his big overcoat, same as always. Ready for next time. If he should need it. And if something happened to him – to Sal – if someone found him, and wanted to give him a decent burial, then all they'd have to do is take that handy spade out of the side pocket of his coat and unfold it and dig.

It draws him closer now until the hum and drone and buzz of it all seems to get mixed into some kind of wailing and he feels himself being sucked over to the edge, to where the grass meets the asphalt, just the way the train used to pull at him when he went to stand next to the tracks that ran out behind the house. Stand as close as he dared while the cars hurtled by and that way it was all noise and confusion and even if he wanted to hear Clothespin Harry and Rosa inside he couldn't. Get right up next to the tracks and feel the cars tugging at him. Feel himself getting sucked right into the thing. Wanting to get sucked into the speed and finality of it. Standing so close the door handles on the freight cars brushed the tip of his nose. If the yardman had left one unlatched for the hobos it might have swung out when the cars lurched so it would catch him on the side of the head and knock him dead or at least unconscious.

Sal on his way in from the woodshed. Spent all day chopping wood for the stove. October moving fast now into November. Leaves gone and the ground hard in the morning, grass matted and frosted under the weight of cold air. Crisp in the morning as he walked to the woodpile and took up the axe to chop. Chop a hole in the day. Climb inside and stay there for as long as you can. Fill yourself up with the swing and chop chunk of it.

Move to the saw. Cut the long pieces down to splitting size. The smell of the pine needles and sap and bark. Chop through a morning with the sun rising high and bringing late October heat. Sweat now, and a drink of water from the well, cool and long and running smooth into your stomach like a river of calm. Stay out here while Rosa and Harry sleep it off, the same as they always do, until they get up some time after noon and start all over again. The rhythm of their day as sure and predictable as the path of the sun across the cold sky. By suppertime Sal thinks it might be alright to go back in. He's hungry and maybe his mother has managed to cook something. Something good. How does she always manage to do that, Sal wonders. Cook something warm and good to eat for him. For Clothespin Harry. How does she manage that?

A meal for Harry. Harry with his delicate hands. Harry with table manners. Rosa has to set his place at the table a certain way. Cutlery just so. Glass there. If she forgets that the glass — the one for the beer he always drinks down at the start of every meal in one long elegant sweep of his hand and elbow, his Adam's apple and mouth in such perfect rhythm you could write a poem about it — goes on the right-hand side, there will be trouble. Sometimes Rosa puts his beer glass down on the wrong side of the plate. On the left side. A mistake she knows she should never make. But something makes her. Something inside the shack that came from out in the woods. Something out there somewhere. To make her do a thing like that.

If Sal catches her mistake and fixes it before Harry has a chance to notice, Rosa takes him aside later and says, "You didn't have to do that, Salazar."

"But I wanted to." He means he wanted to save her. Save them.

"I know you did, and I'm grateful. I should be glad you did. But you know it'll happen anyway, don't you? Whether you do something like that or not. Sooner or later. You understand that, don't you?"

"Yes. But I was just trying to help you. You want me to help you, don't you?"

"Why, of course I do Sal, honey, but you don't have to worry yourself about it all the time."

"I can't help it."

"Listen to me. I don't know if I can make you understand, if I can make anyone understand. I don't know if I understand it myself, but sometimes, it's better just to get it over with. Sometimes the waiting is the worst thing. Sometimes it's harder to wait for what's going to happen than the thing that actually happens. So then you make it happen, and that gives you some power. You can say that you made it happen. That you had some kind of a say in it. Sometimes that's the only way you can get through it. The only way to make any sense out of it. Do you understand, honey?"

"You don't want me to do that anymore."

"Oh, no," and she grabs him roughly and pulls his head to her bosom fiercely. *"No, Sal, that's not it at all. Don't ever stop, honey. Not ever."*

"You're not mad at me?"

"Why no. Not a bit. You're my best and only hope, Sal. My best and only hope."

So Sal keeps on putting the pillow back on the right side of the sleeping bench where it should be. Slides the bottle back to the side of the table Harry will sit on. Wipes the stain off the chair where he sat at supper. Acts like nothing happened. Like he didn't do anything.

But Sal can't do it all. Can't figure out everything that might be wrong. A lot of the time he can't figure out what it is until it's too late. And when Harry spots it, and his eyes get that sparkle, you know it's going to happen anyway. No matter how hard you tried to keep it from happening. And you know that after he's sat for a long time at the table, drinking slowly, deliberately, drinking, thinking,

waiting for elvis

Sal and Rosa watching the concentration in his eyes, like watching a fire, watching and waiting, that he's going to come up with something. When you didn't think it was possible for him to figure another way to hurt you more than he already has. But he always does. Screaming inside yourself to run run run run run run run take Rosa and run run take Rosa and run because a big take and a big take a big and run a big hurt was coming a big a hurt a big hurt was coming for sure a big hurt for sure and for sure it was almost here almost here a big hurt almost here and take Rosa and run run run.

And then Harry, everything settled in his eyes, looking up from the table and saying, "Come here, Rosa."

"No," Sal hears himself say. "Me, Harry. Take me."

"Now you just stay there and watch, Big Son," says Harry, and pulls a clothespin off his hat. "Over here, Rosa. That's a good girl. All the way. That's it. Now sit here on my lap."

Up in his hammock, Sal holds his two hands out in front of him and stares at them under the moonlight that seeps in through the layered boughs of pine and cedar. He didn't spot Little Elvis up at the median today but he picked up some things in the ditch just the same, enough to fill the flour sack he always carries, before he headed into the woods that always take him back. Give him rest. That's what the trees do. The boughs and branches. That's what home does. Gives you a place where you can rest. Completely. Like the cabin in the woods where he and Rosa listened to Elvis out on the crumbling porch before Clothespin Harry found them. That was home. Or maybe it was another place Sal can't, won't, allow himself to remember. Or maybe there never was any place called home.

Sal pulls the coat close around him. Even up in the hammock he keeps it on. Wears it like a second skin. Can't imagine himself without it. It holds everything he needs and more, stuffed into the pockets, inside and out – all of them filled to bursting. He won't sleep now – not for a long time, but dream himself a waking dream. All of them take place on the same quiet country road he always walks down. Always the houses

waiting for elvis

and barns on either side and big cottonwood trees in every yard. And people who stand under the shade of those trees and wave as he walks by. They all know that if one of them should ever need something, all they'd have to do is just call out to him.

In tonight's dream Sal walks by a green field of fresh-cut alfalfa under a blue sky. It's always a blue sky. Breathes in the sweet smell of the hay and spots a farmer out in the field, bent low over a shiny red baler. Sal leaves the road and walks through the alfalfa stubble toward him. The man straightens up when Sal sets one boot down on the tractor hitch.

"What seems to be the trouble?" says Sal, casually, but underneath he always thrills at the sound of his own baritone voice, smooth as honey. He can make himself talk just as well as anyone else in these waking dreams. Better.

The farmer tilts his straw hat back off his white forehead, pulls a red and white polka-dot handkerchief out of his back pocket and wipes the sweat off his face and neck. "Big clump of alfalfa went in," he says. "Didn't see it in time. Jammed the feeder."

"Need a hand clearing it out?" says Sal.

"Done that already, but I can't run it without the flywheel. Sheer bolt got busted off. I usually carry a spare or two in the tool box but I checked just now and I haven't got another one in there."

"Carriage bolt might do," says Sal. He's already taking stock.

The farmer stops long enough to take a good look at Sal, at the great grey coat he's wearing. "Say," he says finally, "I heard of you."

"You have?" says Sal, trying to sound surprised.

"Yep. You're that guy with the coat they talk about. They say you come around from time to time and help people out."

"Is that what they say?"

"I heard you carry just about anything a guy could ever need – stuffed right into the pockets of that coat."

"Doesn't sound possible."

"That true? What they say? That a guy can ask you for just about anything and you'd have it on you somewhere?"

waiting for elvis

"I guess you'll have to ask to find out."

The farmer takes off his hat and dusts it against his thigh. "Well," he says shyly, "if I was to ask if you happen to have a carriage bolt on you, what would you say?"

"What size?"

"Nine-sixteenths. But half-inch would do."

"Too much play," says Sal. "You wouldn't get around more than a few times before it got pinched off."

"Alright. Nine-sixteenths, then."

"How long?"

"Well, three inch is what I use, but it could be longer than that. Just so it doesn't catch on the pitman arm."

"Three inches you say."

"I got a hacksaw. I can cut it down if I have to."

Sal looks up at the sky, reaches into the inside left breast pocket of his coat, shifts his weight around a little as he sifts through the contents. Then a smile crosses his face as he produces a shiny bolt, examines it, and hands it to the farmer.

"Will that do?" says Sal.

The farmer looks down into the open palm of his leathered hand. "Damned if it isn't galvanized, too," he says.

Sal reaches into another pocket and pulls out a nut and the lock washer to go with it. Drops them into the farmer's hand.

"You'll be needing those, too," he says matter-of-factly.

The man reaches up and tilts his hat even farther back from his forehead, mouth open, speechless.

Sal just smiles, then starts back for the road.

"Wait," says the farmer.

Sal stops. Turns. "Something else?"

"Hell no," says the farmer. "I just wanted to say thanks. For all your trouble."

"Trouble?" says Sal. "No trouble at all."

All the way back through the alfalfa stubble and up to the road – with the farmer still looking down into his hand, shaking his head, looking up at Sal, then down into his hand again – Sal can't keep the grin off his face.

"Sal. That's my name," he says out loud now. "My right name." Not Big Son. Only Clothespin Harry ever called him that. Called him Big Son.

Harry, sitting at the kitchen table in his yellow hard hat, three clothespins clipped onto the front — always three — and Rosa, drunk, barely conscious, on his dirty knee. When he sees Sal he pushes the hard hat back so the white on his forehead shows. Rosa has her head down like it weighs too much, eyes sleepy and stupid, staring over at Sal like he's something in a catalogue. They're drunk, both of them. Nothing unusual. Rosa, up on Harry's knee, has one hand around a bottle, the other on Harry's shoulder.

"Why, hello there, Big Son," says Harry. "I was wondering when you were coming back. We've been waiting for you. We've been talking, you might say, your mother and I. And we've got something to tell you. But I've made up my mind I'm not going to tell you, Big Son. I've decided it's better to show you instead. Hey, Rosa? Because that's the best way, isn't it? That way the boy won't forget. Not if we show him. That's how I'm going to get my point across." The way he puts his hand around the back of Rosa's neck makes Sal think something bad's coming. Something awful.

Harry pulls the bottle out of Rosa's hand, takes a long drink, and puts it down on the table. Rosa's still looking at Sal like he's made out of glass. Harry loosens the last few buttons that run down the front of her dress and pulls it open, exposing one of her great, shiny breasts, the dark brown nipple that Sal can remember being warm and sweet and filling up the space between his shoulder blades when he sucked hard and deep on it, the way she sometimes let him.

Harry's hand squeezes tighter around Rosa's neck, until she stiffens, back straight now, pushing that enormous tan breast right out at Sal. "You see, Big Son, this is how we'll settle everything." Harry reaches up and takes one of the clothespins he always has pinned to his helmet, opens it wide, and holds it over Rosa's dark nipple. Just holds it there. "Now," he says, "don't you move, Rosa. You hear me? Don't move. The boy needs to see this. It's going to hurt. It's going to hurt a lot. But you're going to sit there and just let

waiting for elvis

it. Just let it. That's the most important part. Let it hurt so bad. That's what you have to do. And you, Big Son. You just watch."

When Harry finally releases the clothespin he does so very slowly, looking at Sal. Sal looks at Rosa, at the way her face begins to contort and pale around her mouth. When Harry's hand comes away the clothespin hangs free from Rosa's reddened nipple. Harry gives it a flick with his finger. It dangles there like a pendulum. "You see, Big Son?" he says. "This is how it's going to be." And he begins to pull at the clothespin. Pulls it and stretches Rosa's nipple out further and further. Rosa whining and whimpering and shaking on Harry's lap now, shaking with the pain, tears skidding down her cheeks. And when the pin finally slips off her nipple with a snap, and Rosa gives a little cry – short and quick – that Sal has never heard before, never wants to hear again, somehow Sal knows already that he will hear it over and over again, coming up through all the other night noises, up out of all that chaos and confusion.

Harry brings his small, pasty hand – the one he used to squeeze Rosa's neck – around under her armpit and all the way up to her bruised breast, cups the shiny, rounded bottom of it and holds it, gently, lovingly, in the cradle of his boyish hand. Then he takes a big drink from the bottle and instead of swallowing, brings his mouth, full of whiskey, down on Rosa's breast and over the nipple. His head moves around in big, stupid circles for far too long before he brings it away and swallows loudly.

"And this," says Harry, picking up the key from the table, the one for the big brown clock that Sal has used to wind it every Wednesday – first the right one, then the left – "this will be my job from now on." Harry dangles the key between his yellow fingers, swinging it like a little pendulum of its own. "And do you want to know why? Because here's what I'm going to do for your mother. I'm going to be the man that winds your mother's watch." Then he laughs a long, squeaky laugh before he hands the bottle to Rosa and watches her take a big drink from it. "But it's going to be me, see? Just me. Right, Rosa?" He uses the thumb and index finger to pinch ever so slightly on her bruised nipple. Rosa winces, nods stupidly. And Sal? Sal can't do anything but stand there and look at the two *of them. But mostly at his mother. Because there isn't anything else for him to do.*

The deep green boughs of the tall pine trees sway above Sal's hammock. It's midmorning. The heat is dull, even in the shade. Sal lifts a hand. Examines it. So the steel fist didn't come last night. If it had he wouldn't be able to move so easily. Wouldn't know how to go about trying. It's the same way with words. Even long after. The steel fist makes words impossible. Preposterous. Ridiculous. He was sure it was coming. It was so close. Ready to sneak up and catch him full force. Steel-hammer head-pounding impact. Concussion. A blue fist of steel, shiny and terrible, big as a tank, that hurls itself out of a foggy background and strikes him square between the eyes with its dumb, concussive force.

The rush of that destruction. And after impact, the dizzy, frenzied, craze of desperation to become animate again. To claw his way back to life. Like the doe that almost made it across and got its hindquarters smashed by the black Lincoln Navigator. The way she got up and pulled herself into the forest on just her two front legs. The scratch scrape and drag of that will to live. To run, any way he can. From the thing that just now tried to kill him. Not to let it kill him. To refuse to be killed by it.

Sal understands what the steel fist wants to do. Squash him down until it flattens him out like a piece of paper. Compresses him into a two-dimensional world, an endless flat plane where his existence becomes nothing more than a milk-thin white idea. The most important thing – the only thing – is not to let it make him disappear completely. Give himself a chance to get back, so he can wake up, here, like this, lying in his hammock, his exhaustion so complete it's enough just to try and remember how to breathe.

Today he has the memory of burrowing underground, like some subterranean creature, scratching out a maze of tunnels, looking for a way out. To the surface. The light. Running out of room, breaking through walls and into already-existing tunnels dug before. Until there's no place left to dig. Until the walls between the tunnels have become as thin as canvas. Then the collapse. Standing alone in the centre of an enormous hollow cavern. The black shadow of the steel fist coming down out of the high ceiling toward him. Striking him full force across the bridge of the nose, turning the inside of his skull into a clanging banging barrage. The sickening wet crunch of his skull cracking open, the raw sensation of his own quivering brain-flesh tingling in the open air. He reaches up, probes tentatively, his trembling fingers inspecting the chasm, widening even as he touches it. Something thick and warm oozing out, running through his hair, across his temples and forehead, down the side of his face. He gathers some of the liquid onto the tips of his fingers, holds it out before his throbbing eyes. A frothy substance, white and sticky.

But this morning, when Sal raises his two hands out of the hammock, brings them up on either side, presses them to his skull, slides them up until they meet at the top, he discovers that his head is not split open. Nothing oozing out. Only a dream. He'll get up now. Go back out to the highway.

chapter five

IT'S ARTY'S NIGHT TO BOWL SO HE'S LEFT EARLY. He's a terrible bowler, but he goes for the boys and the beer and that's alright with Betty. The game suits them. It's the adult equivalent of every boy's idle pastime. Set up the blocks. Knock them over. Repeat. That's about all the imagination you need. Besides, she doesn't mind the time to herself. She's got the Closed sign out and most of the lights off. If any customers come they'll see her sitting at the table in the booth but she'll wave them on. She's not ready to leave yet. To turn all the lights off. She doesn't want to think of what she's up to as a kind of waiting. She doesn't want to think of it that way. But that's what it is.

It's dusk now and she's looking out the window as the last rays of the sun turn the tips of the highest spruce trees a bright orange and yellow. The wilderness that surrounds the diner is vast and deep and she feels the sulking presence of it most at this time of day. But outside there is always the intrusion of the traffic that never stops. It bothers her that she can't enjoy the desolate beauty of the place in silence. Silence is what it needs. What it deserves. And she can't breathe the crisp bite of the evening air without also taking in exhaust from all those vehicles, so she stays inside and imagines it instead. How far, she

waiting for elvis

sometimes wonders, would she have to wander away from the highway — into the wilderness — before she was entirely free of its contamination? Before the forest went back to its natural state of utter stillness and purity.

The fact that Arty gets such a big kick out of an evening with his buddies has always been a bit of a mystery to Betty, considering he spends every spare minute of the day with them as it is. Every break he gets from working the grill he's out front in one of the booths, talking to the guys he used to truck with. It seems to her the last thing he'd want to do after that is go out and spend the whole evening with them, too, but she doesn't give him a hard time about it — tries not to let the fact that it shows a terrible lack of imagination bother her. She knew that much going in.

"When you find a man with imagination," her mother always liked to tell her, "you've found a rare and precious thing, Elizabeth." That was back when Betty was still Elizabeth.

"It sounds like something terribly valuable," said Betty. She was sitting at the breakfast table, waiting for her mother to serve her a plate of fresh-cut fruit and a bowl of cereal.

"It is. Imagination is something most men have very little of."

"What about Daddy? Does he have one?" Her father had left the house hours ago. He got up very early every morning and didn't come home again until well after dark.

"Your father? He has a wonderful imagination. I wouldn't have married him if he didn't."

"You wouldn't?"

"Of course not. A man without it becomes dull very quickly."

"Even if he's handsome?"

"I'm afraid so."

"What if he's handsome and brooding?" Elizabeth was imagining Heathcliff. She and her mother had been reading *Wuthering Heights* together.

"Even then."

"What about wealthy? What if he's terribly rich?"

"Especially if he's rich. He's a poor man if his mind's a wasteland, Elizabeth. And he'll make yours one along with it."

Elizabeth and her mother quite often spoke to each other this way at the breakfast table. They liked to imagine themselves as the women in the books they read together, having terribly poignant conversations, thinking of things to say to each other that were full of pith and irony. They were getting quite good at it, but it was all about to come to an abrupt end. The future her mother had laid out for them, the one in which Elizabeth grew up to become a fine young lady of education and manners while her mother cast an ever-widening circle of privilege and envy around her, was never going to materialize.

"But how will I know if a man's got one or not?"

"An imagination? Oh, you'll just know. He'll be different from the others."

"Different how?"

"Well, little things, mostly. In the way he acts. The way he talks. It's not easy to explain. He'll make things more exciting for you. More interesting."

"How? Tell me how."

"Well, suppose he takes you for a walk in the woods."

"That doesn't sound very exciting."

"But that's just it. It will be when he takes you. It won't be like any other walk you've ever taken. He'll say things. Do things. Things that make you feel alive. It's difficult for you to understand now, I know, but you will, someday. I promise."

"Will you teach me?"

"Teach you?"

"When the time comes? Will you teach me how to choose a man with imagination?"

"Let's just pray that you have that luxury, my dear. Most women don't."

Betty was still Elizabeth when her father came home very late one night in a state of high excitement. She was in bed by that time, as usual. Her mother never allowed her to wait up. She was very strict on that. Elizabeth would sometimes try to keep herself from falling asleep until she heard him coming in through the door. Something about that gave her comfort. She didn't usually manage it and tonight was no exception. She'd been asleep for some time when she was roused out of her sleep by the sound of their voices – both of them talking loudly in a way that she'd heard before – her mother reproachful and urgent, her father animated and reassuring. She got out of bed and tiptoed down the hallway to the kitchen, listened through a tiny crack in the door. It was as bold as she dared to be.

"It just sounds so foolhardy to me," said her mother.

"It's nothing of the kind. I'm telling you it can't miss."

"I don't see why you have to risk everything we've worked for."

Elizabeth had heard them like this before. Her father eager to throw their future up against formidable odds. Her mother trying to talk him out of it.

"You want me to squirrel it all away somewhere?" said her father. "Is that what you want? That's not what got us here. A man has to have a dream, Ida. Without that he's nothing. He might as well be dead."

"But this. . .dream – it sounds like pure fantasy, George."

"Call it what you like. I'm telling you it's a once-in-a-lifetime chance."

"But we've only just managed to get this far. And now you want to throw it all away on something like this. What about paying off the house? What about that? At least we'd have that. If things didn't work out."

"Do you have any faith in me at all?"

"Let's not start that again."

"Do you?"

Elizabeth wanted to run into the kitchen and take her father's hand in one of hers and her mother's in the other. Tell them to stop. Tell her father she believed in him. In his dreams. Tell her mother that she should believe in them, too. But that, it seemed to Elizabeth, had always been her mother's trouble.

waiting for elvis

She never wanted to believe in anybody's dreams except her own.

"Don't you see that if you go ahead with this now we stand a good chance of losing everything? Do you see that?"

"I've got us this far, haven't I? It takes money to make money, Ida. I know that even if you don't."

"But there must be some other way. Couldn't you hold something back? Think of me. Think of your daughter."

Elizabeth knew better than to interfere. She didn't want to provoke the other side of her mother's personality. The one where she might catch Elizabeth by the wrists in a sudden grip of terrifying strength and drag her into the room at the far end of the hall, lock her inside. Leave her there for hours with nothing to do but wait, knowing that when her mother finally came to let her out it would only be to make her grovel in a humiliating ritual of appeasement and apology.

"Besides," Elizabeth heard her father say, "it's too late."

"What do you mean too late?"

"I've gone ahead and done it."

"What?"

"It's all signed and delivered. The wheels are in motion."

"You didn't."

"I had to act quickly. This is no time for indecision."

Elizabeth heard a chair scrape across the floor and thought she might be discovered. She ran back up to her room, dug herself in under the covers and waited, but she didn't hear anything more. She fell asleep soon after that and when she got up the next morning her father was gone as usual.

Things happened quickly after that. It was only a few days later that she was roused out of her sleep once again. She thought at first it might have been her father coming in. Perhaps he'd slammed the door behind him, although she'd never heard him do that before. No, it wasn't a door. This sound had a different quality to it. Her mother might have knocked something over downstairs. Accidentally pushed over a chair. It wouldn't be the first time her mother got up in the middle of the night to rearrange the furniture. But no, she didn't think that was it, either. The sound had been sharper than that. More final. More like someone had banged a fist against the wall.

Elizabeth wanted to get up and go to the door but then she heard the heels of her mother's shoes hurrying along the rug in the hall. Her mother never wore slippers – only the same style of black leather shoes, in and out of the house, winter and summer. She decided to stay under the warmth of her covers and listen to her mother going down the stairs. Opening a door. The door to the cellar. Elizabeth knew the sound of it. The hollow creak of its hinges. Then it sounded to her as if someone were trying desperately to stifle a scream. Elizabeth imagined her mother with a hand pressed tightly over her mouth.

The scream lasted a long, long time, and when it was finally over everything was different. Things took on a fudgelike quality after that. Elizabeth still heard and saw and felt things, but they all seemed to be taking place inside a thick pool of chocolate. The taste of it was always there after that. On her tongue. A sickly sweet stickiness at the back of her throat. She could never seem to swallow properly. She spent her days swimming ridiculously through darkened rooms filled with the muffled voices of men and women dressed in black. Somewhere in there she was standing next to her mother, the two of them at the foot of a creamy caramel coffin, listening to the indecipherable whispers of a man in robes.

It wasn't long after that Elizabeth went from wearing fine crisp dresses and shiny patent leather shoes to frocks and second-hand runners. From cucumber and lettuce sandwiches to baloney. The girls at her new school were numb and rude with poverty and neglect and worry. They were unhappy and hurtful most of the time and Elizabeth woke up one morning to the realization that she'd become that way, too. That she was a girl in a cheap dress with cheap food in her stomach and a cheap future to look forward to. That the world had lost its sense of promise for her. That she was unworthy even of her memories – as if they had never really belonged to her in the first place.

The house and contents were sold out from under them to pay creditors and they went from living in a fine country home with a porch and swing to a rundown rooming house with no hot water and no privacy. Her mother let herself go. It began with small things – the way she stopped brushing out their hair in the evening, stopped getting her teeth fixed – and ended with the realization that she'd run out of chances. Another man like Elizabeth's father wasn't going to materialize. It was too late. Her courage left her quickly after that and her looks followed close behind, eroded by the endless cycle of cigarettes and drink and worry she had fallen into. Soon she no longer carried herself in the way she needed to if she held any hope of attracting a certain kind of man – the kind that would enhance, rather than depreciate, her vanishing reputation. Soon she was letting herself be picked up by predatory men in smoky bars where she went to drink away her grief and bitterness. She let them buy her drinks and offer her cigarettes and, later, exact their pound of flesh on the bed in the next room while Elizabeth, as always, tried to sleep through it all.

And somewhere in there she and her mother – without ever saying a word – made a secret pact never to talk about the life they had known. To try as much as possible to make it disappear from their consciousness altogether. They understood that it was better that way. Not nearly so painful. Especially since there was no going back. As part of the pact, Elizabeth knew she needed to stop being a certain kind of girl and become another. And so she became Betty.

When she thinks about it now, she isn't sure that other part of her life ever existed. Was she ever really someone known as Elizabeth? Was her mother ever really a beautiful, gracious woman? All she knows right now, sitting here looking out the window of the diner at the gathering darkness, is that Arty never once took her for a walk in the woods and talked to her the way she always imagined her father must have with her mother.

The phone rings and Betty thinks it might be Arty calling to see why she's still at the diner, but the edgy female voice on the other end is one she's never heard before. Then she knows who it is. Knows this is the call she's been expecting for some time now. The one she knew was coming. In a way she's glad to be getting it over with. When it's done she closes up quickly and heads back to town.

"They've got Tony," she says to Arty when he comes in later that night.

"What?"

"Tony. They've got him over at the Public Safety Building."

"Who?"

"The cops, that's who. He's been arrested."

"What? What for? What happened?"

"They didn't tell me much. Something about break and enter."

"Goddammit. What the hell did he do?"

"It gets worse. There was somebody in the house when they broke in. An old man. He's in the hospital."

"Jesus. What do we do?"

"They won't let anyone in to see him tonight."

"Who? The old man?"

Arty looks at her, expressionless. He's always like this in a crisis. She wants to slap him across the face. Slap some kind of meaningful reaction into him. She knows better than to start in about what happens next, but later, in bed with the covers pulled over her, back turned to Arty – just before she turns out the light – she says, "I'm going in tomorrow morning. You'll have to manage the diner without me for a few hours."

On the drive into Winnipeg along the Trans-Canada Highway, she keeps thinking back to an incident that happened when Tony wasn't much more than a boy. How she walked into the kitchen and found him sitting on the countertop, shoulders slouched, dangling those black boots of his over the edge, scuffing the white cupboard doors. She'd told him over and over not to do that, and now he was up there again, letting her know he didn't give a damn what she said. The boots were a pair Arty had brought back for him from Texas. Arty was still trucking

waiting for elvis

back then, on the road six days out of seven. The night Arty gave him those boots Tony took one look at them, picked them up and disappeared into the other room. When he came back in wearing them, the look on his face had changed. Like he'd figured something out. Discovered something about himself. Something she and Arty would never have any part in. He wore those boots day and night after that – from the moment he got up until the moment he went to bed. Even though they were three sizes too big and looked ridiculous on him. He literally grew right into them.

And there he was, deliberately dangling them over the edge of the counter, knowing she didn't want him up there. Knowing she couldn't stand him doing that. Scuffing up the cupboard doors that way. Betty told him as evenly as she could manage to get off while he smiled back at her defiantly. She knew she had to get him off there – that if she didn't it would all be over. She grabbed him squarely by the shoulders and tried to pull him off. He lashed out at her with a clenched fist. Caught her across the jaw. Sent her reeling back a couple of steps. She came at him again. Grabbed both of his shirt sleeves and yanked as hard as she could. Pulled him hard to the ground while he kicked at her savagely with those boots. He got up quickly when she let him go, looked down at his shirt where she'd torn it open. Then he smiled and put a hand up to the corner of his mouth. Pointed at hers.

"You're bleeding," he said.

Betty put her fingers up to her lips, brought them out in front of her. Saw that there was blood on them. Terrified with anger, desperate with hope, she thought it might be enough to make him leave it alone now, but he took a slow, deliberate step toward the counter. Betty clenched her fists. Set her shoulders. Tony stopped, then turned, and without ever taking his eyes off her, walked out through the open door of the kitchen. Betty couldn't seem to move for a long time after that, and when she finally did, it was only to get herself up the stairs and into the bedroom, where she closed the door before she sobbed into her hands.

waiting for elvis

She remembers that day as the first time she finally faced what she'd sensed from the very beginning. Hardly a day had gone by since Tony was born that it hadn't nagged at her. This thing she never wanted to admit to herself. That her own flesh and blood had never really been hers at all. That her son was never going to let her love him the way she wanted to. Needed to.

It's not something she can talk about. It's too personal. Even the tarot card reader sensed as much. The one she went to see on her last trip into the city to check on her mother. There was a little shop on West Broadway she always passed after she'd parked the truck to walk to her mother's rundown apartment. The sign hanging over the sidewalk always caught her attention. It was a painting of a tarot card. An orange and black wheel with strange symbols on it surrounded by animals that looked like they came out of a book on mythological creatures. Below the picture the sign read, "Tarot Cards Readings. Please Come In." She'd never done anything like that. Felt a little foolish even as she opened the door. A tiny bell tinkled above the door and a slender, tired-looking young woman came out of the darkened back room.

"Reading?" she smiled thinly.

"Yes."

"Come."

The woman led Betty over to a small booth and pulled the curtain, then sat down across from her. She took up the deck of cards from the middle of the table, handed them to Betty with long, ringed fingers.

"Shuffle," she said.

Betty took the cards. They were awkward to handle. Twice the size of regular cards.

"Alright," said the woman after a few moments, and took the cards back from her. "The question," she said. She seemed a little bored.

"The question?" said Betty.

"Yes." Or maybe she was just sleepy. Betty wondered if she'd woken her from a nap. "What is the question?"

waiting for elvis

"I don't have a question."

"You must have a question."

"I see. Well, I don't really know."

"You came for a reason."

"I suppose."

"That reason is the question. Here." The woman turned over several cards and laid them face up in a neat row on the small cloth-covered table. "Pick," she said.

"Pick?"

"Only one. Take your time."

Betty looked at the cards. Thought they were interesting to look at but she couldn't really understand what they were depicting. They didn't seem to be about anything to do with her. With her life. It looked like everything had happened a long time ago. Finally she picked up a card with a young man in armour, wielding a sword and charging into battle on horseback.

"Your son," said the woman. "You want to ask me about your son."

Betty felt a pinch at the back of her neck. All of her guilt and anxiety and shame suddenly seemed exposed to this woman. After that the woman began to lay more cards out on the table in a pattern. She announced each one and talked about what it meant. Betty had trouble concentrating. There were so many cards and so many things the woman said that made sense or didn't, but then she said, "This is the last card," and placed it down on the table. It was the same black and orange wheel Betty had seen on the sign hanging in front of the shop. "The Wheel Of Fortune," the woman said. "Reversed. Events unfold in a surprising manner."

"Surprising how?" said Betty. She felt a small twist below her stomach.

She waited. The woman seemed a little ill at ease.

"Light comes from dark."

"That doesn't tell me much." Betty felt suddenly bolder. "There must be more."

"A transformation."

"How? A transformation how, exactly?"

"This ends the reading."

"Can't tell me any more?"

"Twenty dollars," said the woman and pushed herself up from the table. Betty thought of holding back the money to try and get more out of her, but the exhausted woman looked like she might collapse at any second.

After she'd paid and left she walked along the street for a few blocks, past her mother's apartment. She wanted to think about what it all meant. Try and make sense of it. She wanted to go back and shake the woman by the shoulders and make her spell it out. But instead she turned back and climbed the dilapidated stairs of her mother's apartment and rang the bell.

And now, as she makes her way through the downtown traffic on her way to the Public Safety Building, she wonders if maybe the tarot card reader got it wrong. If maybe it was never supposed to be about Tony at all, but Sal. Thinks that maybe fortune tellers can make mistakes too, like everyone else.

Inside the building a uniformed officer shows her into a small room, asks for her purse, then empties the contents onto a bare table. While she inspects the items, Betty watches Tony through the one-way mirror. He's sitting in the next room. The only furnishings are a wooden chair on either side of a table. He looks so completely alone. Vulnerable. For a moment her heart is full. My boy, she thinks. They've got my boy. He looks as alone as Betty has ever seen him. All his defences seem down. She wants to run in and take him into her arms like she never has in all those years raising him and tell him everything is going to be alright. But she won't. Can't. It's too late for that. Besides, he'd never allow himself to be handled that way. It's been like that from the earliest moments of his life. Betty could never hug the doubt and confusion out of him. Doubt that turned to bitterness. That has made him so willing to cause trouble.

This isn't the first time Tony's been in trouble with the law. She and Arty have made all the rounds with the social workers and psychologists. Put up with all the looks from the teachers and principals at school. Jumped through all the hoops with the probation officers and lawyers and priests. It's been one thing after another with him right from the start. For as long as she can remember he's been getting into some kind of trouble. She could never understand how it happened that he got so bad so fast. Where it came from. All that anger. All that meanness. Like he had it inside him from the day he was born – before even – the way he'd kick at her from in there, not like he just wanted to let her know he was there, but like he wanted to hurt her. Make her cry. Making her cry is what Tony has always done best. That smirk on his face when he finally succeeds. Like there's victory in it. Where did that come from? Arty was never around much, but he was a decent father. Never mean. And Betty hasn't been a bad mother. She's always done what she could so he'd turn out good. But he hasn't. It's like he was carrying something around inside him right from the start, and all she could do was watch it grow in him along with his arms and legs and hands.

But this is the worst. He's gone too far. This time, she knows, he's going to jail. He's used up all his last chances. She knows all this but she still hates to see him sitting there like that. Her boy. She hates to see her boy in a place like this. It would be different if he were sick or hurt. Then she might be able to find a way to help him. Nurse him back to health. Make him better. Get him out of this place. Free of these people. There's a smell to this place. It's hostile. And where they'll send him is sure to be worse. It'll bring out the worst in him.

The officer hands back the purse and opens the door to the other room. Motions Betty in. She walks in and sits down across from her son. The officer stands at the door, arms folded.

"Your father couldn't come," says Betty.

"Did numbnuts call you?"

Betty knows he means the lawyer. "No. Not yet. Has he been in to see you?"

"No. That's why I'm asking, for Chrissake."

"I guess he must be busy."

"Fucking goof."

"You know I won't stay if you talk that way."

"This whole thing is a joke."

"I can't stay long anyway," says Betty. "I have to get back to the diner. Your father's all by himself."

"Did you bring me something to eat? Some real food at least? The stuff they serve in here tastes like shit."

Betty had thought of packing a few things for him, but just at the last minute decided not to. She's only now discovering why. Even as she sits here, across the table from her son, looking into his snarling features, she understands what she has to do.

"Listen to yourself," she says.

"What about smokes? Did you bring me some more smokes?"

"Listen to the way you talk."

"Huh?" On his face is a mixture of annoyance and boredom.

"You know why you're in here, Tony?"

"It's not my fault that clown I got for a lawyer hasn't got me out of here yet. And what good are you?"

"Nothing has ever been your fault, has it?"

"What?"

"And nothing ever will be. Isn't that right?"

"What the fuck is your problem?"

"You, Tony. You are my problem. You and your attitude are my problem."

"Jesus, Ma, you're starting to sound like all the rest of them. You're supposed to be my goddamn mother, for Chrissake."

"Am I?"

"You're supposed to be on my side."

"Which side is that, Tony?"

"What the fuck is that supposed to mean?"

"Tell me what it means to be on your side."

"Jesus," he looks over at the cop. "My own fuckin' mother."

"I'm tired of trying to make you feel better about yourself. I'm through."

"I don't believe this." He bangs a fist down on the wooden table. "Fuck!" A few small chips of white paint flutter down onto the floor.

"Blaming everyone else for your problems is as easy for you as breathing, isn't it?"

"Shut up, Ma."

"It's always someone else that's supposed to pay for your mistakes. Isn't that right? Isn't that the way it works?"

"I said shut up. Just shut up."

"You're no good, Tony." Betty is up on her feet now, purse in her two hands, surprised to hear herself saying all this so clearly, so freely. For the first time.

"Ma?" Tony looks up at her. She has never seen him look so frightened.

"I can't save you this time. And I don't think anyone else can. Not the lawyer. Not the social workers. But that isn't the worst thing. The worst thing is that even when this is all over and you're back out again you'll cause more trouble. You'll do it because it's all you know how to do. There'll be heartache and sorrow wherever you go. Your whole life is going to be one long endless river of shit and I'm not going to swim in it with you. Do you understand? Tony? I refuse."

"Ma?"

"I'm going now."

"Ma, don't do this to me."

"I have to get back to the diner."

"Look. I'm sorry. Stay. Please? A couple more minutes? Please?"

"Tell me something to make me stay, Tony. I'm listening." Betty clutches her purse, waits. Tony slouches back in the wooden chair. Stares up at her. Finally, he pushes the chair back and looks over at the officer. Then back at Betty. He breathes a deep sigh and gets up slowly out of the chair.

"I gotta piss," he says, and walks away lazily into the other room.

chapter six

IN HIS DREAM – THE ONE SAL WOKE INTO JUST NOW instead of the other way around and that's what threw him off – he was lying in his hammock, eyes open, clear-headed and refreshed and feeling as good as he could ever remember, listening to complete silence. Not the sneaky kind that comes after the steel fist. Different this time. Not frozen. No slow maddening thaw, numbness thick as sludge in his skull, pain bleeding into his eyeballs, hammering against his ears, every cell in his body frozen, blood crystalized. This time he got right up out of his hammock, pine needles crunching under his feet. Not stiff and sore from all that paralyzed effort. Muscles fluid and bold.

When he emerged out of the forest the sun was just up over the trees, air crisp and fresh like he'd never smelled it before. And there, before him, were four lanes of smooth black asphalt, and not a single vehicle as far as he could see in either direction. Not one car. Not one truck. Sal walked down into the ditch and through the grass, greener than he'd ever seen it, each blade shiny and new and beaded with dew. He made his way up onto the shoulder, then the first lane of asphalt, knelt on one knee and placed a hand on the surface, the road cool beneath his

waiting for elvis

palm. Tried to grasp the situation. Get hold of this impossible idea. This altered reality. No traffic. None at all. The highway deserted. He stood again and looked leisurely up and down the long length of black ribbon, first in one direction, then the other. Perfectly empty.

He began to walk down the road, slowly, not in a rush, not in a hurry, the way the traffic always made him want to with its bustling, bullying insistence. There was time now. Time to take it all in. That was when he noticed the animals standing at the edge of the woods. First a young doe. Then a racoon. Next a fox peeking out through the trees. All of them looking out at the highway. The young doe was the first to step gingerly out of the woods, stop, then cross carefully through the still grass, climb the embankment and place one hoof carefully down on the asphalt. Sal understood that for her – for all the animals – this was a ribbon of death. Of pain and suffering. But now the doe was walking across the blacktop, the clop of her hooves echoing hollow, like amplified water droplets plopping into a rain barrel.

The next to leave the cover of the trees was the fox, who sauntered, head up, onto the road, then trotted lightly up and down the quiet length of the pavement, sniffing the air, lowering and raising its muzzle. Soon other animals joined them on the cold black surface. A pair of ravens hopping awkwardly and calling out to each other across the median. A family of grouse pecking at loosened pebbles imbedded in the asphalt. A badger waddling fat and low along the white centre line. A lynx pouncing at nothing, then rolling over luxuriously, rubbing its back into the hard black roadway. Some animals seemed to want to do nothing more than stand still for a long time in one place, just to feel the surface of such an unfamiliar world beneath them, look up at the sky as they did so. Without fear. And Sal walked among them. Took a few tentative steps in one direction, then another.

Before long the highway became a blacktopped playground. Animals were chasing each other about, some running in quick dashes and bursts in every direction, others in circles, still others

waiting for elvis

sprinting along its length, all of them in love with the smooth, hard surface, the solid footing, the clear lines of sight. So open. So clean. But then the young doe stopped abruptly. Sal saw her muscles tense. She sniffed the air and snorted, punched her two front hooves loudly down on the asphalt, and bolted off into the trees. She must have heard something, thought Sal. Smelled something. Something must be coming. The other animals stopped too, senses on full alert, before they disappeared swiftly off into the surrounding woods until, in a matter of seconds, the roadway was once again entirely deserted.

And then Sal saw it. A small dark figure in the distance, shimmering up out of the warming asphalt. Something coming toward him, a little larger now, walking upright. Something apelike. Hairy. Naked. Closer now. A creature walking with purpose and rhythm. It's coming for something, thought Sal. Now he could make out the slope of the shoulders, the hair-covered torso, white teeth. "It's him," Sal heard himself say. Little Elvis, striding rapidly toward him, had grown from a baby into a boy, arms thicker now, swinging freely at his sides, chest bulging with sinewy muscle. His hands were much bigger too, hairy, fingers curved into claws, nails long and visible. He was clutching something in one paw. It hung there limply, like newly killed prey. Something small and pale and delicate. An animal of some kind. But there was no fur. Must have skinned it, thought Sal. Little Elvis, still walking swiftly, raised his arm slowly out in front of him, held the quarry up for Sal to see. Held it out to him. And Sal could see clearly now that it wasn't a skinned animal at all. It was a baby. A baby made of pink and red and blue blotches. Little Elvis was closing fast now, moving with surprising speed. Sal could make out the creamy white of his eyes now. The black purpose at the centre of each. He turned and ran down the length of perfect asphalt, legs pumping hard, but he could feel Little Elvis gaining on him. He needed more speed. Threw off his greatcoat and watched over his shoulder as Little Elvis leapt over it with frightening animal stealth. He could hear the slap slap slap now of hairy feet on the blacktop, the distance

waiting for elvis

between them closing fast. Then hot breath on the back of his neck, the smell of it rancid in his nostrils. A huge hairy hand clamping down on his shoulder. A terrifying, powerful grip that pulled him down, crashed the back of his head onto the black asphalt. Then blue sky above, Little Elvis holding the baby for him to take before he slipped into unconsciousness and just now woke up, back here, in this morning of jangle and stink, to the familiar wall of noise pushing in through the trees.

Sal opens his eyes to look up into the boughs, blue sky sprinkled above them, and welcomes the taste of gasoline and diesel exhaust acrid on the back of his tongue. The closeness of all that tonnage hurtling past sends a slight vibration, a subtle tremor up into the trees and through the conduit of his hammock. And this morning, it all comes as a relief. He gets up out of his hammock, strides quickly through the trees toward the highway, stops at the edge of the forest to take in all that noise and filth, thankful to be standing here, knowing the rest was just a dream. Such comfort in the tyranny of the traffic. But he can't push it all out of the way. Not the part where Little Elvis tried to make him take the baby. Take the baby and bury it.

Later, out in the open, walking the ditch, the steel fist hovers low. Sal tries to count a convoy of thirty-wheelers. Three sections of dollies that's two-three-two a set of two and a set of three on the front trailer two more on the back that's seven duals for fourteen and the other side is another fourteen that's twenty-eight add the front two that's thirty. Another. Then another. The trucks hammer away at him.

Sal in the hallway crouched low like a hunter, knife down at his hip, clutched in both hands, watching Harry. Eyes fixed on his back. Harry asleep on the bench, his lizard back turned toward Sal, one flap of his greasy overalls undone and brushing against the floor. Sal studies the rhythm of his breathing. Waits for the one, deep breath when Harry takes all the air inside the room into his lungs and holds it there for what seems like forever. Then move. And just when he finally lets it out again – fouled now – that's the time. Do it then.

waiting for elvis

Sal got the knife at the J. C. Penney store the last time they were across the line in Walhalla. Paid for it with the money he's secretly been stealing out of Harry's wallet. A bill here and there, but only when there's enough so Harry won't miss it. Bought it special because the blade is longer by six inches than anything in the kitchen drawer. That's important. And it has to be very sharp. Sal's made sure of that, too. Honed the edge carefully with the same stone he always uses for the axe, out in the workshop. When Sal was done sharpening the knife, he drew the cutting edge lightly across the back of his thumbnail. It left a clean white line. He thought of using the axe itself to do the job. Split Harry's skull open with it. But what if things went wrong and it was a glancing blow that didn't kill him, or even knock him unconscious? No, this is better. More final.

Sal's plan is to sneak up from behind and plunge the knife deep into Harry's side, just below the shoulder. That's the spot. One deep, killing stab. It will have to be that way. There won't be a second chance. Punch the blade through Harry's overalls and into his chest, between his ribs, through the lungs and into the heart. Even so, Harry's liable to make a grab for something. For Sal. Put him in a death grip. Strangle him even as he himself dies. But he won't get the chance. Sal will jump back, like a cat, and stay out of Harry's reach. Then watch him struggle, clutch and grab at air. Wait. Sal knows how to wait.

Sal's been practicing on the cow carcass down in the gully whenever Harry's not around. It's been there for a while now, lying next to the frozen creek. Harry would have slaughtered it for meat, but it'd been dead for too long by the time he found it. "Animals will take care of it," he said, and left it there. But the animals haven't touched it. It looks the same as it did when it was alive, lying there on its side, except that its bloated stomach is frosted over.

Sal wants to do it like the African warrior he and Rosa saw at the matinee movie in the Walhalla Theatre last spring. That was just a dance, but Sal remembered the way the tall lanky black man held the spear, lunged forward, stabbed, then jumped back. That's what I'm going to do, he thought. That's how I'm going to do it. Practiced it just that way. Lunge forward. Stab. Jump back. Sal *stabbed the frozen cow so many times there was no place left to try, and so he brought a length of rope out from the shed and tied it around the cow's legs, winched it around a tree and pulled, by inches, until he had the cow rolled over on its other side. Then he filled that side up with puncture marks, too.*

Sal wants to do it after Harry lets out the long breath because that way his lungs will be empty. The chest cavity will be smaller and the knife won't have as far to travel to reach the heart. And if Harry has time to take in another big breath, so he can get up and come across the room to kill Sal, his lungs will just fill up with blood instead.

Today Harry got up early and did the same thing he does every Sunday – sat at the kitchen table and whittled a new clothespin for himself. Fashioned a new spring for it, too, from a spool of heavy wire he always uses. Harry can make a clothespin so stiff when he clamps it on you it's like the jaws of a devil dog biting into you. Or one so easy you don't think it's ever going to cause you hurt until it comes so quiet, from so far away, like a thin black fog.

This morning Harry whittled the two wood pieces out of basswood, pale and smooth. Pure white. No two are ever alike. Some thin and elegant, others thick and chunky, tapered into points, sometimes with ridges and serrated edges. This one had a row of tiny, sharp teeth running in a line the length of each piece. When he was done making it, he clipped it to the bill of his construction helmet and went to sleep on the wooden bench at the end of the hall.

That's where he is now. Sal's mother is out on the porch, in her rocking chair, sleeping off the booze and pain. Sal's been watching Harry for a long time now, and still no big, deep breath. What if Harry doesn't take one today? Will Sal have to wait until next Sunday? Roll the knife back up in the same white cloth and take it out to the woods and bury it under that same pine tree again? Dig it up next Sunday morning?

Sal wonders if Harry's coveralls and the skin underneath will be anything like the cow's hide. The first few times he tried to penetrate it with the knife, he was surprised how much force it took. The cow didn't want to let itself be punctured. Sal had to learn how to throw

waiting for elvis

his weight in behind his shoulders and channel it down into his arms and through his hands. Make his entire upper body rigid so he could use all the muscles there to focus his strength on the point of the blade. All the energy has to go there. All his power has to find its way to that target. The point of the blade. After a while Sal learned how to make the knife go in up to the hilt every time and still have enough agility left to jump back quickly.

But what will Harry's reptile hide be like? How tough will it be? The knife will have to penetrate the thick, greasy fabric of the overalls, then the three or four shirts he always wears underneath, before it even gets to his lizard skin. Sal doesn't want to think about what will happen if the knife just bounces off. Or the blade breaks, and Harry turns from his sleep and figures everything out in an instant.

"Time is coming, Salazar," his mother used to say sometimes.

"What time is that?" Sal would always ask, even when he knew the answer that would follow.

"When I won't want you here." They'd be sitting out on the porch, his mother in her rocking chair and Sal with his head in her lap, waiting out the late afternoon heat.

Sal would lift his head off her lap. "You won't?"

"No. I'll want you gone."

"But why?"

It was always when Harry wasn't around that his mother would get to talking this way. He would have left midmorning in his pickup truck. There was never any telling whether he'd be back in a couple of hours or a couple of days. Sal would set up the record player and they'd go sit out on the porch where they could hear in time to run in and get it out of sight before Harry came in. By that time Sal had learned to keep it in a box, hidden out back of the woodshed, and only take it out when they were sure he'd be gone for a while. And that's when his mother would start in about how Sal would have to leave one day. How one day soon she would send him away for good.

"When that day comes," his mother would say, "and it will, you head east, Sal. East. And never look back."

"East," Sal repeated for her, because he understood that she needed him to do that.

"That's right. And keep on going. No matter what happens. No matter how scared or lonely or hungry you get."

"If you try to come back there won't be any chance for either of us. You understand, don't you?" She'd lift Sal's face in her tanned hands and look into his eyes. "You have to walk and keep walking and no matter what happens you have to never never look back."

"I will." He could never resist the words that came next. "But Harry will find me."

"He won't."

"He said so. No matter where we went. Remember? He said he'd find us and hurt us worse than ever."

"Not if I stay here."

"He'll hurt you for sending me away."

"I'll say I tried to stop you. That you ran away."

"That won't matter. Not to Harry."

Sal would put his head back in his mother's lap for a moment, then lift it back up when he thought of something else. "What about setting up the record player? And putting the needle back to the beginning when the time comes? Who'll do that?"

"You don't have to worry about that. I can take care of that just fine."

Sal had managed to splice the machine back together after Harry kicked it across the room. There wasn't much left of the frame, but that didn't matter. He'd reattached the wiring to the needle and found a way to float the broken arm over the record with a length of copper wire. It skipped too often and the sound came out a little warped and wobbly but it was still Elvis singing "Are You Lonesome Tonight?" In his fury Harry had failed to break that record, only chipped off a piece like a bite out of a cookie so you had to start the needle almost halfway through and Elvis was already singing, " . . . *chairs in your parlour seem empty and bare. . .*"

waiting for elvis

"What will happen to you?" Sal asked. "When I'm gone?"
"Why nothing. Nothing at all."
"What will you do?"
"Same as I've always done, Salazar."
"But what if you came, too. We could both go. Take the truck. You know how to drive it now. Just take it and go. We could head into the States and I'd get a job picking apples in one of those orchards you told me about. You could rest in the shade and I'd bring you a big juicy apple to bite into and then at the end of the day we'd take the money and buy more food and get you a bottle. How would that be? We could do it like that."
"No, Sal. It has to be just you. Alone. And don't forget."
"Forget what?"
"East. Head east."
"Why that way?"
"Because he said to send you down that way."
"Who did?"
"Why, Elvis, of course." His mother was always telling him how Elvis would come to her in dreams. Spoke to her just the way she was talking to him now. "He said he'd take care of things when you got out there."
"Out where?"
"He promised me."
"But how will I find him? How will I know where to look?"
"You don't have to worry about that. He said he'd find you when the time came."

There was a long silence after that, the two of them listening to the needle crackle and hiss at the end of the record, crickets chirping under the boards of the porch floor.

All day Sal walks the ditch until, at dusk, he bends over another cardboard box, lifting a corner of the damp, flattened paper that's worked its way into the soil. They somehow manage to do that. Flatten out and bond themselves to the ground, half-rotted, camouflaged by grass clippings. There could be almost anything under a box like that. How many hundreds has Sal pulled up out of the dirt? And always he discovers the same thing: disfigured stems of grass tangled into a flat mosaic of pale tendrils, coiled and spiralled into each other in a desperate attempt to find sunlight. And always the delicately curved trenches of worms and beetles, cleanly carved into the moistened soil. Sometimes a small rodent that scurries when Sal curls away the softened paper, sometimes the sudden buzz of a hundred flies out of a jiggling mound of white maggots. It always amazes Sal that these tiny perfect creatures – worms so packed with juicy life and energy, so shiny and new, should breed inside the remains of a rotted carcass, something that got buried, became flattened out into the two-dimensional world of the dead. That's the other thing that's always there, mixed in with the smell of damp earth and decay. The smell of the grave. Of death and burial.

Sal bends low, kneels over the box, pulls gingerly at a flap. He can't help himself. He has to know what might be underneath. Inside. He has to do that every time. Even when he knows it couldn't possibly be the same box. The Oreo Cookies box with the blue letters along the side that Rosa said to use. Even when he can see that this box is nothing like that. Bigger. A different colour altogether. It doesn't matter. Something draws him. What if it should be that box? The one he used that night. Somehow it turned up here.

Sal peels back the rotting cardboard. Nothing to see but some night crawlers squirming into hiding, a black beetle scurrying under the pale luminous grass, and that smell. The damp smell of the grave. Sal lifts the rest of the box away and carries it out in front of him over to the edge of the pines. Sets it against a tree to dry out and in a few days he'll come back and take it over to the pile with all the other boxes, hundreds of them, all stacked into a rounded mound of slow musty decay. Someday Sal would like to make a big fire. Burn them all. Someday when it's been dry for a month and there's no wind and he can watch all those mistaken boxes, all those imagined possibilities, go up in flames. But not yet.

The steel fist is hovering low over his head. Sal hurries back to his place in the woods. Climbs up into the hammock. I'll dream myself a dream, he thinks, and then he's on that same country road where everyone smiles and he smiles back as he walks along and whistles. A white-haired woman sitting on the front porch of a white house calls out to him.

"Just a moment, young man," she shouts.

Sal stops on the road, puts one hand on each lapel of his greatcoat, looks over at her. "Good morning, ma'am," he says. "What can I do for you?"

"You're that man, aren't you?"

"Which man would that be?"

"They say there's a man walks these roads that carries everything in his coat. A coat just like that."

"That so?"

"They say he's got everything a body could possibly need right there in his pockets. You wouldn't be that man by any chance, would you?"

"Well, ma'am, it just so happens I would."

"Well then, I wonder could you help me. I'm sewing up the hem on this dress here."

"That's a pretty dress."

"It's for my granddaughter, Elizabeth."

"She'll be lucky to have it."

"And I just now ran out of thread, wouldn't you know. I've got more in my sewing box but it's just so far to run all the way back into the house and up the stairs to fetch it."

"No need for that, ma'am."

"No?"

"Sewing thread you say."

"That's right."

"And just what colour would you be needing?"

"Why white. Plain white thread. Would you by any chance have some on you?"

"I believe I do, ma'am," says Sal. "I believe I do."

"I'd sure appreciate a small length. If you can spare it, that is."

"Would that be polyester or cotton?"

"Polyester, I suppose. If you've got it."

Sal goes to reach into a pocket of his coat to pull out a spool of white thread. Hold it out for her to see.

"Well bless my soul," she'll say. "It's all perfectly true."

"Ma'am?"

"What they said about you."

"How much did you say you needed?"

"Another arm's length or two should finish the job."

"Let's make it two, then, shall we?"

"That would be fine."

"Two it is." Sal will pull off the thread, bite through it with his teeth, and step up onto the porch. Hold it out to her. "There you go, ma'am."

"Oh, that's wonderful. Thank you so much." She'll take the thread from him with a shiny, translucent hand.

"Glad to do it, ma'am."

"I hope I haven't been too much trouble to you."

"Why, no trouble at all, ma'am. No trouble at all."

She smiles up at him. "You're a kind and generous young man."

But when Sal reaches for his coat pocket there's nothing there. He looks down to discover that he's not wearing the coat. Runs screaming.

"Wait," the woman calls after him.

But Sal has entered another dream. In this one he is back out on the deserted highway. He can't help himself. The enormous silence draws him just as strongly as the crush of noise does in his waking hours. Draws him out of the pines, across the clean grass and onto the perfect black asphalt, so smooth he wants to lay down flat on his back, curl his shoulder blades against it. Lose himself in that long, hard plane, stare up at the dense blue sky of heaven. Lie there, listen to the animal noises, the clopping hooves of deer and antelope, the scrape of a raven's claw, the scratch of a snake's belly. It's morning in the dream, and the asphalt is invitingly cool. No sun overhead to bake the blacktop into softness. No heat yet to boil out the stink of oil and tar and rubber. Only the smell of fresh-cut grass on either side, lush and green. Sal walks in his bare feet, luxuriates in the tickle of the tightly curled blades between his toes. Back up on the roadway he feels the clean asphalt like a mild abrasive under the pads of his feet, like a volcanic beach, or a boardwalk Rosa once took him down – or did he dream that, too?

But now the animals scamper off in a sudden panic and leave him alone to stare at a figure rising out of the heat waves just beginning to form in the distance. A creature, growing larger, on him so fast he has no chance to get clear but runs straight down the road away from it. Not into the pines. The road becomes his only means of escape. The only way to try and put some distance between himself and the thing he fears most.

Little Elvis, muscular, hairy, swift and dangerous, teeth bared and closing fast. But this time he's carrying something in his two clawed hands. A box, half-rotted, falling apart, with blue letters along the side. Something dangling out of it. Something that might be a tiny arm or a leg. Something dark dripping onto the black asphalt. Sal running now. Little Elvis holding the box out to him, grinning with those white fangs, urging him to take it. Sal trying so hard to escape, whites of animal eyes on him now, a hairy hand on his shoulder, claws digging into his skin, pulling him down. Down.

Rosa, lying on the bed, under the soiled covers, waving him over after she called him into the room.

"*Take it out to the woods, will you Salazar?*" *she tells him.*

"*What is it?*"

*His mother holds a box out to him. A box with blue letters on the front that spell "*OREOS.*"*

"*Here,*" *she says.*

"*What's in there?*"

"*Take it.*"

"*What is it?*"

"*I want you to bury it.*"

"*Bury what?*"

"*Out in the woods.*"

"*Now? But it's dark out.*"

waiting for elvis

"You have to do it now. Would you do that for me, Salazar?" Her weak, tired eyes plead up at him.

"Alright."

Sal takes the box from her. It's not clothes. Too heavy for that. It's not newspapers or magazines. Too light. Something that's compact. That doesn't fill up the whole box. He turns to go out through the door.

"And Salazar?"

"Yes?"

"Don't open it."

"I won't."

"Promise?"

"Promise."

"Just give it a decent burial. That's all."

"I will."

"I'm so tired, Salazar, so tired."

"You rest now."

"Go." She waves him to the door. "And, Sal? I want you to come back and tell me when it's done. When you've finished. I'll wait. Can you do that for me?"

Give it a decent burial. That's what his mother said to do. It's important to do that. Carry the box under one arm, spade out of the shed in the other, up to the clearing in the woods. Start digging after you've put the box down on the frosted ground. Stop when you think maybe you hear something. Something mixed in with the sound of the pointed blade cutting into the cold black earth, mixed in with the grunt and groan of your effort. Something like a small muffled thump against the side of the box. Just a clump of dirt that rolled there off the spade. That's what it must have been. Start in digging again. Pretty soon something like a timid scratch, a small animal scratching inside the box, trying to get out. You stop digging to listen. Wait. Hear only silence. But when you go back to work there it is again. Something shuffling. Rustling.

Hole dug now. Good and deep. Stop to lean on the spade. Stare over at the box. Wonder should you open it. Even though Rosa said not to. Stand quietly. Watch. Listen. The way you do when Harry

waiting for elvis

and Rosa are in the next room and it gets so quiet after Harry's done and you wait for the slightest sound of a floorboard creaking on the far side of the door, stare a hole into the doorknob waiting to see if it will begin to turn, ever so slowly, slowly. That's how you stare at the box now. Wait to catch the slightest movement, the faintest rustling. With every hair on your body singing.

Only one thing to do now. Tear himself out of the hammock and run headlong to the place where he's hung up all that metal and glass and plastic. Run into that garden of pain full tilt and keep on running until what's on the outside starts to feel like what's on the inside. Make it cut. Make it bleed. The first thing he hits is the torn and mangled frame of a destroyed motorcycle that spins away from his impact and sends him stumbling sideways into a gas tank ripped apart in an explosion. The sleeve of his coat snags on a ragged edge of metal and he tears at it, stumbles backward into a car door that swings wildly and sets a dozen other objects in motion. A crankshaft comes out of nowhere, clips him on the side of the jaw and rocks him like a hard jab, staggers him for a moment. He gathers himself and sprints hard into a heavy driveshaft that splits a gash in his skull, spins and reels and the coat catches again – a pocket this time that tears open and spills out its contents. He tackles a chrome bumper, then a rusted muffler, then lunges wildly at a transmission housing that crushes the muscle and bone of his shoulder and still he will not stop. Pieces of fabric hang loosely from the coat and catch on every sharp piece of metal. Another pocket explodes into a thousand carefully collected and catalogued items that scatter across the forest floor. He keeps at it until the ground beneath his feet is littered. Until the precious coat has been all but torn away from his body and all that's left is a ragged collection of shreds and patches. Finally, he takes aim at a tire rim hanging dead-still before him. The impact sends it careening away from him in a long arc. When he spins around, it swings back and hits him full force from behind. Knocks him hard to the ground. He staggers to his feet, reeling like a prizefighter, knees buckling, head down. With the last of his strength, he tackles a truck axle that cracks his skull hard enough to knock him unconsciousness, collapse him face-first into the chaos and confusion beneath his feet.

chapter seven

WHEN HE STAGGERS INTO THE DINER, ARTY'S IN THE kitchen turning on the deep fryer and Betty's lifting a tray of cinnamon buns up onto the counter after unlocking the front door. Sal stumbles through it and braces himself against one of the tables. Betty runs up to catch him before he falls, calls for Arty even as the first trucker pulls his rig noisily into the parking lot.

Arty hurries out from the back and, when he gets a look at Sal, says, "Jesus H. Christ. What the hell happened to him?"

"Get the pickup," says Betty. "We have to get him to a doctor."

But Sal reaches out, clutches at her shoulder, shakes his head, gulps desperately at her, tells her no with his eyes.

"Come on," says Betty to Arty. "Help me get him into the kitchen."

"Aw, Christ, we don't want to do that. The place'll be hopping in ten minutes. Can't we just call an ambulance?"

"Goddammit, Arty. Are you gonna help me or not?" Betty puts one of Sal's arms around her shoulder and tries to straighten him up. Starts across the floor.

"Alright, alright," says Arty and jumps in under Sal's other shoulder. They help him into the cramped kitchen and sit him down on the makeshift cot in the corner where Arty sometimes likes to grab a quick nap. There's a worn wooden desk next to it with paperwork piled high and an old leather chair pulled up to it. They lower Sal onto the cot and Betty sits down in the chair, says to Arty, "Get the first-aid kit out of the cabinet."

"Jesus, do you have to do that? What about we just call the cops and let them take care of it."

"And bring me some towels, would you?" says Betty.

"Goddammit," says Arty, and does as he's told.

"And put some water on to boil," she shouts after him and looks down at Sal. Sees the blood rising in his cheeks, his pale blue eyes beading up with moisture. Sees the mixture of pain and fear there. "It's alright," she says. "Nobody's calling the police or a doctor or anyone else. I'm going to get you all fixed up. So just relax."

Arty sets a basin of water down next to her, and she begins to clean the wounds with a damp cloth while he looks over her shoulder. Blood from several deep cuts on Sal's head has trickled along the back and sides of his neck down into his shirt.

"That one looks like it could use a stitch or two," says Arty.

Betty uses a butterfly bandage on it, works with a deep concentration. When they hear the trucker coming in through the door Betty gives Arty a look that tells him what he needs to do. He disappears into the front. When he's gone Betty looks into Sal's eyes and says, gently, "We have to get these off." She means the last few fragments of Sal's shredded coat, and the tattered shirt beneath it. She pulls them both off carefully and when the naked shoulders and torso have been exposed she tries not to notice the musculature. But in spite of herself, she can't suppress a small rising inside. It is such a surprisingly good chest, muscular and smooth. She wills herself back to the task of inspecting bruises and scrapes and cuts – some raw and red, others blue and black, yellow and green. All shapes and sizes, all the colours of the spectrum. But they are almost exclusively limited to his upper body, as if whoever did it was not allowed to hit below the belt. Some

waiting for elvis

show the imprint of the object that must have inflicted it: straight-lined like a length of pipe, elegantly curved along an arc of bent steel. The contours and shapes of weapons Betty can only imagine.

She's thinking back now to that first time he came in. To the cuts and bruises in various stages of healing she saw then. How she had a vague sense then that they were not the result of any accident. That they had been inflicted by some other force. And now something else comes harder to her – the strong sense that he has somehow done this to himself. She can sense it in his mannerism. In the way he watches her tend each wound. She can't imagine it, though. Unless he buried himself, waist-deep, directly in the path of an oncoming avalanche. An avalanche of hard steel and broken glass and jagged metal.

"You just about done with that crazy bastard?" says Arty from the grill. He's busy shuttling between pouring coffee out front and cooking up breakfast orders in back. "Place is starting to fill up." He flips a couple of eggs and looks over at her. "I could sure use a hand."

Betty doesn't bother to answer. Goes back to tending to the wounds. She knows Arty will be alright. He can cook bacon and eggs and make toast and coffee, though not usually all at once. But he'll manage. He sets two plates up on the service window and starts around to the front.

"What happened?" she says to Sal. "Who did this to you?" It's hard to tell how much of the discomfort in his expression is from the pain and how much is from her questions. "Sal," she says. "Is that right? That's your name, isn't it?" She gets up and empties out the basin of pink water into the sink. Refills it with fresh warm water. Adds a little salt from the shaker on the counter. Sits down again on the chair next to him. Goes to work on his wounds again.

"It's him, isn't it?" says Arty the next time he comes in. Betty looks up at him. "It's that same crazy son of a bitch that was in here last time. Am I right?" He's at the grill now, cracking eggs onto the hot surface. "I want him out of here as soon as he's cleaned up." He drops four slices of bread into the toaster. "Goddammit, Betty, we got a business to run."

Sal looks over at her when she places a small bandage over a cut next to his bloodshot eye. He winces in pain but tries to smile at her. She finds herself enjoying the process immensely. She likes the feeling of it. This laying on of hands. Something about it feels very important. She doesn't want it to end. She imagines an infinite number of wounds on Sal's body. Herself as an indefinite agent of healing. Please, God, thinks Betty, don't let Harvey bring in a busload of seniors now.

She takes up the cloth again and washes away a little of the blood that has trickled down across Sal's chest, where a few small curls of hair grow. The skin is smooth but firm where she runs the damp cloth over it. She does the same for his wide, solid shoulders. His well-developed biceps. It was different when he had the greatcoat on. All this surprising masculinity is distracting and disturbing for her.

"How did this happen?" she asks. "Can you tell me?"

Sal tries to shake his head no. Nod his head yes. Make her understand. It's not that he can't. Not that he won't. He never sat down and made any such pact with himself. Never to utter another word. Nothing like that. It was never that kind of affliction. That simple. He can't remember exactly when he lost control of the decision or how it became so foreign to him. For a long time now he has lived in exile, in a place where there is only the never-ending process – the infinite moment – of not making the choice. To speak or not to speak. In between. Caught. Constantly on the verge of saying something. Of not saying anything. A billion words in his head. A vast storehouse of utterances. Waiting. Cued-up. Backlogged. Or an empty chasm devoid of even a single syllable.

Betty is wrapping the last of a gauze bandage around Sal's ribs when – slowly, deliberately – he reaches out and lightly cups one of her breasts in his large sculpted hand. She stops, straightens a little. Keeps her eyes firmly fixed on the middle of his chest, where her hand rests against the white gauze. Without raising her head she gently grabs him around the wrist and – just as slowly, just as deliberately – lifts his hand away and lowers it, palm down, onto his thigh. Then she reaches for the strip of white adhesive tape hanging from the desk beside her and fastens it in place. She does all of this with her thighs held tightly together to try and hide the trembling there.

She wills the tingle between her legs to pass just as Arty walks in from the front and looks over at them. She can see he has no idea what just happened. When it comes to anything between her and Arty there hasn't been much to get worked up about for a long time now. In the earliest days of their marriage there were times when he'd come home after a couple of weeks on the road and they would go at each other pretty hard on the couch or in the bedroom. But that died out after Tony came along, and since then things have pretty much dried up. The most she can hope for now is Arty getting up a hard-on after a couple of stiff drinks before bed and mounting her matter-of-factly as soon as they get under the sheets. He fucks her quickly and efficiently and spends himself with the same kind of nervous energy he uses to fix the deep fryer or hose down the back concrete pad. He comes in two or three short spurts, pulls out quickly and rolls off onto his back as if he were excusing himself.

It's easy enough for Betty. She doesn't have to do much more than lie there – doesn't want to do more these days. He's small enough for her to take him in without too much discomfort, even though she's never really ready. She's resigned herself long ago to the reality of not being filled up the way she needs to be. Once in a while she has a few drinks of her own and tries to get something going but it's never much good. Whenever it happens he makes it clear he really doesn't want her doing that kind of thing. More than anything it seems to scare him a little when she gets that way. He has no idea what to do with her. It might be something as simple as Betty pushing her hips back up at him as he thrusts into her. Lifting him up off the bed with her pelvis, just a little.

"Jesus, Betty," he says when she does that. "Can we just do this thing?" Then she lays back and lets him finish and after he's pulled himself out and rolled over with that small grunt of his it's only another minute or two before she hears the long even breaths of his sleep. So after that it's okay to cry and use her fingers and finish. It's been like that for so long now Betty can't remember another way. But still there's that place inside her where something more needs to happen. She hasn't completely given up on it. She's not ready for that yet.

When she's got Sal all cleaned up she gets one of Arty's work shirts out of the corner closet. He's always got a few extra in there. Goes through two or three a day what with grease and dishwater and sweat. She takes it over to Sal and sits him up for a moment to get it on him. It fits him a little tight around the chest and shoulders, and the sleeves are too short, but after she's rolled them up for him and tucked it in it looks fine.

"There," she says. "Good as new. Are you hungry? Let me get you something to eat." When Arty comes back in she's handing Sal a plate of eggs and toast.

"Christ, now we have to feed the poor bastard, eh?"

Betty looks up at him. "Yes we do, Arty. That's exactly what we have to do." Then she looks back down at Sal. "I'm going out front for a bit, but I'll check in on you in a little while, okay?" She gives Arty one more look before she disappears through the doorway. When she's gone he glances over at Sal and says, "I don't know what you're up to, pal, but you're not fooling me. Not for one damn minute. I seen your kind before. You're not as helpless as you make out to be, isn't that right? And you're no dummy. You can't pull that stuff on me. So don't even try it. You try anything. Anything at all."

Sal looks over at him the whole time he's talking and doesn't move. Eats his eggs and toast and chews down the food without moving any other part of his body. Arty goes back to working the grill, thankful he can stay here now and just do the cooking and Betty will take care of the rest, but the next time he looks over Sal has fallen back onto the cot. When Betty comes back she hurries over to check on him, sees that he is in restful sleep, and leaves him there.

waiting for elvis

He sleeps all the rest of that day and over Arty's protestation they leave him undisturbed. When the supper rush is over and they're getting ready to close, Betty comes in and finds him sitting up.

"That was a long sleep you had. You must have needed it. How are you feeling?" There are no more customers out front so Arty doesn't put up much of a fight when she helps Sal through to the front and sits him down in the booth nearest the door, then settles in across from him.

"Is there someplace we can take you? Someplace you need to go?"

"Yea," says Arty from behind the counter. "Like the funny farm, maybe."

Betty gives him a look.

"Is there someone we can call?"

She sees now that his attention has been caught by something else. He seems transfixed by the sight of the great German coat – the one her father brought back all those years ago – hanging on the rack next to the door. He can't take his eyes off it. She gets up and takes it off the hook, brings it over to the table and lays it across the Formica. Sal fingers the material, slips a hand into one of the big pockets. And right then and there Betty makes up her mind. She gets up out of the booth, takes up the coat.

"Here," she says, motions for Sal to get up. "Put it on."

Sal looks up at her, unsure.

"It's alright," she says. "I've been looking for a good reason to get rid of this thing for a long time now."

Sal gets up and puts his arm into one of the sleeves just as Arty steps out of the back. "Hey," says Arty, "what the hell do you think you're doing?"

"It's alright," says Betty, still looking at Sal and not at Arty. Her eyes let him know it's okay. He puts his arm into the other sleeve and Betty slips the coat over his wide shoulders. Then she turns to Arty. "It's my coat," she says. "I can do what I want with it."

"But that's no ordinary coat. Goddammit, Betty, you're not gonna let him take it are you? A guy like that? And you're gonna let him walk out of here with it?"

97

"A guy like what, Arty?"

"For Chrissake, Betty. You know what I mean. We'll get him something else. I'll find him something back at the house."

"We don't need to find him anything else." She smiles up at Sal and smoothes the material across each shoulder. "This will do nicely."

"Jesus, Betty, if I didn't know better I'd say you were in love with that halfwit."

"Don't listen to him, Sal. He doesn't know any better." And now she looks at Arty hard. "Do you?"

"Aw for Chrissake, Betty."

"Do you?"

"I gotta finish up in back."

"Do that, Arty."

When he's gone she says to Sal, "What good is a coat if no one gets to wear it, eh?" and smiles up at him.

Sal would very much like to talk to Betty. Try to thank her somehow. He would like to try and tell her how things are, too. How they got that way. But before he could do any of that, before he could get himself to say anything at all, he'd have to let it all go first. All of it. And that's something he just can't do. It's not safe. It will never be safe to do that. How could he ever make it safe to tell anyone about the steel fist? How could he ever make anyone understand about that?

Betty has her hands on both sides of the coat now, pulling the lapels together, fastening one of the tarnished brass buttons across the front. Sal looks down at Betty's hands.

"Don't listen to Arty," she says. "You hear? Don't ever stop coming. No matter what happens. You hear me, Sal? Don't ever stop coming here. Promise me?"

She hands him a silver metallic Thermos of coffee. A paper bag of sandwiches.

Sal feels like he might choke. Something is making his eyes water. Sal holds the Thermos very tight in his hands. It shakes. It vibrates. It shines.

chapter eight

BETTY'S IN BEHIND THE COUNTER WAVING A MENU slowly back and forth in front of her, trying to move a little air across her neck and face. They're in the middle of a heat wave and this is the hottest day yet. The place is air-conditioned but the truckers like it on the warm side so Arty keeps turning it down. When she complains it's always the same exchange between the two of them.

"The customer's always right, Betty."

"The customers aren't the ones running around working up a sweat, Arty. And what about you back there over the grill? I don't see how you can stand it."

"Heat doesn't bother me. Never has. Besides, it's a win/win situation for us."

"How do we win working in this heat, Arty? Explain that to me."

"That's the beauty," he'll say. "Keeps them happy and saves us a couple of bucks on the hydro bill."

Arty's at one of the booths now, talking to a couple of truckers. They're going on about what the heat is doing to their rigs: the refrigeration units, the tires, the engines, the brakes, the livestock they're hauling – the list goes on and on.

"No sign of any let-up either," says one of the men at the table with Arty.

"Supposed to keep on like this right through the weekend."

"Cattle are losing ten percent of their body weight just on the trip in," Betty hears one of them say. "Same with the poultry."

"Producers don't like it. Fill 'em up with water before they ship but it doesn't do any good."

"Some of 'em are trying to sell dressed instead of live weight but the packers aren't going for it."

"Pigs don't feel it so much for some reason."

"Hide's different. No fur. No feathers."

They talk about the heat and drink their coffee. That much doesn't change. They still want their coffee, no matter what the weather. Even when Betty offers them a nice tall glass of iced tea, they turn her down. Stick with what they know. She tunes out their conversation but she can't help thinking about her mother, up in that squalid apartment in Winnipeg, coping in this heat. She probably hasn't even bothered to turn on the air conditioner Betty had Arty install in one of the windows a couple of years back. That was after Betty walked in and found her so weak from heat exhaustion and dehydration that she forced her into the truck and drove her to the emergency ward at the Health Sciences Centre. They took one look at her and admitted her. Hooked her up to an IV for a couple of days to get her system back to normal. Her mother doesn't feel the heat the way most people do. Same with the cold in the winter. With everything. Betty thinks it must be because her body is so full of booze all the time. Numb. So she can't feel any of the things that are killing her.

The heat is killing people in the city. Betty hears about it on the news every morning. Reads it in the paper. Wonders why it is that it always seems to happen to people in the city. Is it hotter there? What about a place like the roadside where Sal spends his days? It must get damn hot there. All that heat from the asphalt. The engines. What about a place like that? And him with that

waiting for elvis

big coat. The German soldier's coat she gave him to wear. Arty's been riding her about that. Ever since the heat wave began. Getting in his digs.

"That coat is sure going to come in handy in weather like this," he'll say. "Sure wouldn't want to be caught out there without it." Stuff like that. Betty doesn't pay much attention. She imagines him retreating into the cool shade of the forest, maybe making his way down to the river, where it would be even cooler. She's not worried about Sal.

But she can't get the image of her mother in that apartment out of her head. People dying all around her. In the other suffocating rooms. And out on the streets. In sweltering back alleys and on steamy sidewalks. Betty knows she could call but even if she did it wouldn't mean much. Most of the time her mother doesn't bother to answer the phone. Same as she doesn't bother to open a window. Wash her clothes. Comb her hair.

Betty's anxiety about her mother has lost some of its edge over the years. The intensity has gone out of it. The kind of worrying Betty does now has a kind of numbness to it. It's been too many days and weeks and months of torture. Too many years since she was dropping off groceries at the apartment regularly, food her mother would leave untouched on the shelf or in the fridge so the next time Betty came over there was the stench of rotten fruit and meat and vegetables making her gag as soon as she stepped in through the door. Those were the days of endless pleadings and meetings with social workers and people from AA, of Betty dragging public health nurses over to the apartment so her mother could swear and throw half-filled glasses of rum and Coke at them from across the room.

They're long past all that now. Down to a few phone calls a month. A quick visit every now and then, just to drop off some cans of soup or a tin of coffee. Stay ten minutes. Get out. That's about all Betty can take anymore. Still, times like this she hates the idea of hearing about her mother on the news. Wonders if it could really happen that way. They'd try to notify the next of kin first, of course, but a while ago Betty had to change the phone to an unlisted number to keep her mother from calling at all hours of the night. It was the only way to put a stop to the senseless alcoholic rages, the terror-driven bile her mother would spew at her through the phone line in a voice that didn't even sound human. So how would the police know who to call? If they did find her mother dead in the heat?

"It just doesn't seem right," Arty says to her on the drive home that night. "Her being left alone to live like that."

Betty made the mistake of mentioning something about her mother. Knew she shouldn't have bothered. The way things are between Betty and her mother isn't something she can really explain to anyone. Certainly not Arty.

"I know. I'm such a cold-hearted bitch. That's what you're thinking, isn't it?"

"All I'm saying is maybe now's the time to patch things up with her. While you still have the chance."

"Patch things up. Simple as that. Nothing to it."

"You know what I mean. Before it's too late."

"Too late? Too late for what?"

"You know."

"No. No, I don't. Tell me Arty, too late for what?"

"She's your mother, for Chrissake."

"Same as Tony's your son."

"What the hell does that mean?"

"I think you know what it means."

"Look, all I'm saying is she needs help."

"Really? I had no idea."

"Seems to me like you're worrying about the wrong people. That big dumb bastard that's been coming in here. What do you want to worry about a guy like that for when you got people right here – right under your nose that need looking after. All I'm saying is I don't get it."

"I tell you what, Arty. You just worry about yourself, same as you always have, and I'll worry about everybody else. That suits you, doesn't it?"

Arty doesn't say any more after that but the next morning,

after she's got the soup on the stove and the cinnamon buns out of the oven, Betty gets in the pickup truck and heads for the city. On her way in she drives with the windows wide open. Lets the noise of the engine and the tires and the wind rushing past her ears drown out the cheesy AM radio play. Checks the roadside for any sign of Sal for the first few miles, until the rocks and trees of the Shield give way to open sky and wheat fields and the highway settles into the flat, wide crawl of the prairie.

"It's like an oven in here," she says when she walks into her mother's apartment. The windows are closed. The air conditioner is off. Her mother is sitting in the same chair she spends all her days in, the burgundy fabric threadbare and smooth across the back and on the armrests. The television is on, turned up too loud as always.

Betty walks over to the window air conditioner. "It must be a hundred degrees in here." She turns the knob awkwardly. "Why haven't you got this on?" The unit kicks in noisily. "You could at least open a window."

The room is a squalid tangle of bottles and cigarettes and garbage. The ashtray — the same orange onyx monstrosity she always uses — is stuffed to overflowing with cigarette butts. Betty brought over a couple of smaller ones from the diner once but her mother refuses to use them, says the big one saved her life and she'd use it again if she had to. The varnish of the coffee table top is a scarred mosaic of cigarette burns and dust. The kitchen counter is cluttered with half-empty bags of white bread, some of them green with mould. Open cans of food sit here and there, spoons sticking out of them.

"There. Doesn't that cool air feel good, Ida?" Betty doesn't use the word mother anymore. Hasn't used it for a long time. Not since back when she was Elizabeth, actually. Their relationship now is wrapped up in so many indignities and sufferings that it would only sound contrived. Ridiculous. "Have you been eating anything?"

It's late afternoon, so Ida will just have started into the serious drinking. She's wearing the same threadbare cotton slacks she dresses herself in every day. The same stained cardigan sweater. Tattered fur-lined slippers. She looks up at Betty for the first time. "You leave me here to rot in this rathole. And then you come around for five minutes and act like you care." Her hair is bedraggled and grey. She no longer bathes her skinny, emaciated body. Or brushes her rotting teeth. "What kind of a daughter is that?" She lifts a half-empty glass to her lips.

Betty heads for the kitchen. "I'm going to clean up a little in here."

"No daughter at all if you ask me."

"After I've done the dishes I'll run some water and you can have a nice cool bath. How would that be?"

"I know what you're up to," says Ida.

Betty swears she will not be drawn into the usual kind of exchange. The one she's hacked her way through too many times before.

"You want to punish me."

She knows how much she will hate herself for letting it happen. Hate that she couldn't keep herself above it.

"It's those dolls, isn't it?"

Her mother can still press all the right buttons to make her forget that she doesn't have to do it. That she can refuse.

Betty is at the counter now, running a sink full of hot, soapy water. "When is the last time you had a nice bath?"

"You've never forgiven me for that."

The dolls were the last thing Betty had allowed herself to hang on to. The last vestige of her old life. The one in which she was still Elizabeth.

"If it wasn't for those stupid dolls we might not be here now. Like this. Did you ever think about that? Did that thought ever cross your mind? If your father hadn't spent all that money on them."

She'd had three shelves of them in her room. Some of them were very expensive and she had heard her mother scold her father on more than one occasion for his extravagance. Not that he didn't bring back fine things from his business trips for

waiting for elvis

her mother, too. But it was always the dolls her mother seemed to go on about. That's the way Betty remembers her father. As always, just back from a trip or getting ready to leave on another one. She can never remember a lot of time in between, only that the dolls her father lifted out of his suitcase and placed in her small hands became a kind of barometer for her, each one able to forecast whether his short stay at home would be stormy or fair.

And then, not long after he died, her mother started asking for them. By that time she'd sold off most of her jewellery, the china, the good furniture. The contents of the house had become her bank of last resort. And now she was selling the dolls, one by one, to a collector. Forcing her daughter to take them off the shelves and hand them over. Elizabeth understood how much her mother needed the money – not for groceries or a new pair of shoes for Elizabeth, who had grown out of hers – but out of desperation to continue living a life that was slipping away from her faster than she wanted to admit. And each time she looked into her mother's aristocratic eyes, saw the suffering there, she found it impossible to refuse.

Still, she managed to keep one to the last, after all the others were gone, the one that resembled her – Elizabeth – most. The last one, her namesake, she kept back as long as she could. It was a little girl doll, small and delicate, wearing a bright blue dress with white lace trim and tiny white patent leather strapped shoes. Her hair was auburn, like Elizabeth's, perfectly textured and made out of real human hair. The doll's face and hands were porcelain, hand painted, with delicate features and blue eyes to match the dress. The skin was olive, criss-crossed with fine, barely visible lines. The hands, impossibly tiny, were perfectly formed, fingers curled just so.

Her father had placed it into her outstretched hands after one of his trips, the way he always did. "Watch," he'd said, and as she held the doll with both hands, he tilted it over on its back. The eyes closed, then opened again when he tipped it back up. She'd looked up at him, smiled, looked back down at the doll.

Put a single fingertip up to one of the small glossy eyelids, pulled it down, let it flip back up. It became her favourite thing to do when she secretly played with the doll. When she thought it was safe to do so. She repeated it over and over. Endlessly. Never seemed to tire of it.

Elizabeth liked the way Lizzy's dress tucked in tightly at the waist, with a sash that tied around the back in a bow. It was exactly the kind of dress she herself liked to wear back then. The doll was small and delicate and she hid it away hoping her mother would think there were none left, but it didn't do any good.

"You know I wouldn't ask if it wasn't absolutely necessary." Her mother was standing in the doorway, arms folded, waiting for her to turn over the doll.

"I told you, there aren't any more."

"I'm sorry, Elizabeth."

"It's true, Mother. Honestly."

"You know this isn't easy for me. You understand that, don't you?"

"But I've told you. They're all gone."

Her mother just stood there looking at her, daring her to keep lying.

"But why Lizzy, Mother? Can't I just keep Lizzy?"

She could see the frustration building behind her mother's eyes, but she'd made up her mind to take a stand. This was the last doll and she was going to put up a fight.

"Where is it?" said her mother, fingers pressing deeper and deeper into the pale skin of her upper arms, lips growing thinner.

"Where's what?"

"Goddammit, child." Her mother brought both hands down at her sides and clenched them, body rigid. It was the first time her mother had ever sworn at her. Elizabeth hated the way it sounded. Cheap and ordinary.

"I haven't got it," she said, which was technically true. The doll was hidden away where her mother would never find it.

"Get it."

"I won't."

"You know how much we need the money."

"How much you need it, you mean." Elizabeth was surprised to hear herself say this.

"I don't deserve that."

"Don't you?"

She had never defied her mother this way. Had always given in to her elegant authority. But now there was something about her transparent neediness, her vulgar frustration that made Elizabeth want to disobey.

"What do you want from me?" said her mother.

"Nothing. I don't want anything."

"You want me to beg? Is that it?" There was a trembling in her mother's voice now and Elizabeth saw the will draining out of her face, as surely as if it were her own blood, saw how weak and small she suddenly looked, and lost all her anger.

"Go to the kitchen and wait."

"Fine," said her mother, with as much dignity as she could manage, and disappeared down the hallway.

Elizabeth waited until her mother was out of sight before she took the doll down out of the closet, freed it from the box she'd hidden it in. She walked into the kitchen with it, held it out to her mother, tipped on its back, so the eyes would be closed. Her mother took the doll formally and smiled.

"I'll get us both something," she said.

Elizabeth shook her head.

"A hair clip. What about that? A nice brass one for your beautiful hair." She reached out to run a hand up through her daughter's fine, long hair. Elizabeth pulled back. "Wouldn't you like that?" Elizabeth knew there would be no clip. Knew her mother would spend the money on herself, the same way she always did. Every penny of it.

"It's alright. I don't need anything," she said. Not because it was the thing her mother wanted to hear. It wasn't that. It really was true. Somehow, from the time she'd taken the doll out of

waiting for elvis

the closet to the time she'd given it over, she'd made up her mind never to need anything from her mother, from anyone, again. To live her life in a new way.

"You know I'd never do a thing like this if I didn't have to."

Elizabeth stood, hands at her sides, looking out through the doorway of the kitchen. She could see both of them reflected in the full-length mirror that hung at the far end of the hallway. Something about her mother from behind, sitting in the chair, the doll in her hand, made Elizabeth look at her in a whole new way.

"It's easier for you than it is for me," said her mother. "You're young. Being poor isn't so hard for the young." She was holding the doll in both hands now, looking down at it. "But it's different for me. It's harder. You can understand that, can't you, Elizabeth? It's just so damn hard."

"You have to call me Betty from now on."

"What?"

"I want you to call me Betty."

"Betty? Don't be silly."

"I mean it. I won't answer if you don't."

"You're serious."

"Yes."

"But why?"

"Because that's who I'm going to be from now on."

Her mother suddenly scrunched up her face and squeezed small bright tears out of her eyes. "Oh, Elizabeth," she sobbed, "that's so awful."

Betty wanted to cry too, but she didn't. She'd seen it all in the mirror just now. Seen it in the way her mother sat, back slouched, in the barren kitchen. The way the two of them looked in that light. They would lose the house soon, she understood, and with it the last vestige of their privilege. They would be forced to take a small, shabby apartment in town and begin the dull, daily ritual of life without money. And this was part of the plan Betty had for how she would manage it. How she would find a way to forget old habits, the big and little

waiting for elvis

indulgences of that former existence. The first step was that Elizabeth would become Betty. She was going to be a teenager in another year, and by that time she'd be able to do pretty much as she liked, because by then her mother would have lost the rest of her courage and, along with it, all her charm. She would become ineffectual in every way, a woman who no longer took an interest in her daughter's schooling, public as it was, in her suffering with dresses too small and shoes too cheap, with fending off surly boys who wanted her to come out with them for all the wrong reasons, who stalked her rapidly changing body with their forceful, oversized hands, grasped awkwardly at her new hips and breasts. Betty saw all of this in that moment, in the mirror's reflection.

"What is it?" said her mother. She was looking up at Betty now. "What are you looking at?" She must have seen it too, then, because she sat back, with a blank look on her face, and neither of them said anything more.

Later, after her mother had dressed and left to go sell the doll, Betty shut and locked the door to her room. She lay down on the bed, rested her head on the fluffy white pillow, looked over at the lace curtains on the window. She knew it would be the last room she'd ever have with curtains like that. She got up and spread them wide, pulled up the ornate window sash as high as it would go, stood for a long time, staring out at the cold dark, taking in great gulps of crisp autumn air, swallowing down her new and unpleasant future.

When Betty thinks about it now, she isn't exactly sure how she managed to make it into adulthood, but she did. She doesn't want to try too hard to remember the details. The idea stirs in her a small sense of dread, even now. Leaves her wondering about the decision she made all those years ago. To forsake her identity. Deny all her longing. Wonders if it was ever really possible to live a life without want. Without need. And she isn't so sure any longer that it was really such a good idea to let herself become this way. And then, as she watches her mother pick up the glass of rum and Coke sitting on the table next to the sofa

waiting for elvis

chair and drink deeply, she finds herself wondering whether now might be a good time for her to stop.

"I had as much right to those dolls as you did." Ida lights a cigarette. Coughs. "I had a right."

"You want me to say that I forgive you?" says Betty. "Is that what you want?"

"I don't give a damn about your forgiveness." Her mother turns to look up at her. "You think you're better than me." She holds up the glass of brown liquid, allows herself to examine it, makes a great show out of swirling it around in the dirty glass. "Just like your father. That was always his problem. And you're no different. He left me. Abandoned me. Same as you. Cowards. Both of you."

Ida takes a big drink out of the glass. Drains it. Reaches for the bottle that is always just an arm's length away and fills the glass halfway with rum. This seems to give her new strength. "What good was he? When it really counted. What good are you?" Her mother turns her head away for a moment but not before Betty can see a single tear start out of the corner of her eye. Her mother rubs it away roughly. Sits silently for a moment. Betty is thinking about how she read that sometimes certain traits skip a generation. It was one of those books on child rearing. One of the countless she scoured to try and find some reason why her own son was so unreachable. She's thinking now that it might be true. That in many ways Tony and her mother are alike. Something in the genes. Something that got passed on. Inherited. Something unexplainable they were born with. A willingness to let the world beat them, and, at the same time, to live in the fantasy that they were winning. That they were somehow victorious.

chapter nine

ARTY'S OUT BOWLING SO IT'S JUST BETTY sitting across from Sal, watching him eat in that quiet way of his. She can tell by now when he's had a bad night. Sees it in his eyes. Sees how he's gone too far inside himself again, become lost. How he's fighting to get back out. She wants to help but Sal doesn't give her much to get hold of. He's barely there. Parts of him never seem to be there, even on the best days. She's never seen the part that makes him want to talk, not to her anyway. Whatever it is that's happened to him seems to have swallowed up all the words with it.

He takes in the food with a complete lack of urgency. Eating for him seems to be not so much about consumption as nourishment, which makes him different from the other men that come into the diner. For them it's all about swallowing things up. It might be the food Betty serves them or the conversation they take part in or the sliver of cleavage she gives them access to or the miles on the road or the diesel in their tanks. It makes no difference. It all comes down to the act of absorption. Of personal gravity. Pulling things toward you. At you. Into you.

If Arty was around Sal might still have come in, but she would have had to coax him inside. Betty can sense he under-

waiting for elvis

stands Arty doesn't really want him coming around. He's careful not to wear out his welcome. Never stays for very long. Arty's mostly in the back cooking, so that makes it easier. But Betty can tell Arty is biding his time. Waiting for something to happen. For somebody to do something, say something, that will give him the reasons he needs to put an end to these visits. But for now he's content to allow Sal to come in and sit down in the booth at the far end – always the same one – and wait for Betty to bring him a nice cup of coffee and a fresh cinnamon bun.

A rig pulls off the road and two men come into the diner. They're regulars. Hank and Henry. Big men with big appetites. She knows they're going to want to eat. She gets up and heads in behind the counter, lifts a pot of coffee out of the machine and picks up a couple of menus. When the two men pass Sal in the booth they give him a good looking over as they walk by, then settle into a booth of their own farther down. One of them says something to the other that makes him snicker a little.

On her way over, Betty shoots a glimpse at Sal, sees the way he's drinking his hot coffee in small sips, never looking up at the men, never making eye contact. It's always like that. It would have been easier if they'd chosen to sit at the counter. That way they'd have their backs to him. But the kind of men who do that usually come in alone. Don't care to mix with the others. They sit with their backs hunched over, pay serious attention to their eating and drinking and smoking. They pay with a smaller tip and get back on their rigs and drive off.

While Betty pours the coffee the usual exchange takes place. The small talk that is always part of the ritual – predictable and safe. No imagination needed. It requires only a selection of pre-screened responses and quips that she could execute in her sleep. Men who come in off the road like this are not interested in having a real conversation. That isn't what they're here for. All they want is a little break from their isolation. Their loneliness. They just need someone to pay a little attention to them. All the better if it's a woman who's got a little something to show. Arty tried to explain to her once how the highway can make a man lose himself. Make him forget he's made of flesh and blood and bone. Betty didn't bother telling him that she feels that way every morning when they make the drive in from Hayden. How the sameness of it all gives her a dull, edgy headache. It hits her that she can't remember the last time she had a real conversation with anybody.

She understands these two men are talking to her in exactly the same way they will talk to the next waitress in the next diner a few hours later. That they're no different than any of the other truckers she deals with all day, every day. Their lives are a predictable sequence of rewards and punishments. The whole time she's talking to them she's thinking how she's pretty sure Sal has a good imagination. She can see it in his eyes sometimes. Sense it in his mannerisms. He's more of a thinking man than anybody might guess. She wonders if these men would think it funny if she told them it was Sal – yes, the grubby-looking bum in the overstuffed army coat sitting over there – and not either of them, who somehow manages to make her think of herself as feminine. Who makes her feel like a woman.

When she's done looking after them she comes back to the booth and. before she sits down, places something small and shiny black on the table in front of Sal.

"It's a CD player," she says, and sits down across from him. "Do you know what that is? It plays music." She takes up the two small earphones, holds one up to each ear, then hands them over to Sal. He takes them from her. "Go ahead," says Betty. "Try it."

He puts them in and she presses the Play button.

"If you don't like that kind of music," says Betty, "I can get you plenty of other stuff. I don't think you'd care much for any of the stuff Tony had. It's all the same. Like fingernails on a blackboard."

Sal is listening to a woman singing softly and sweetly in his head. There are strings and a guitar and it sounds fine, but nothing like Elvis.

"That's Tony's player you got there," says Betty to Sal. "I figure he bought it with my money anyway, so I'm entitled to it.

waiting for elvis

He left it when they took him. Said he didn't want it because someone would just take it off him as soon as he got in there."

Tony won't be coming into the diner for the next little while. It was never to lend a hand anyway. To stay only as long as it took for Arty to give in and hand over some money or blow up at him and send him cursing out through the door, swearing his way across the parking lot and back onto that motorcycle. Betty thinks it's just as well. She doesn't miss how the truckers would look at each other and mutter over their coffee cups about the kind of son she and Arty were raising. Easy for them to criticize. Riding across the country all week in their fancy rigs while their wives are back at home trying to hold things together on their own. Easy for them to come back to the house for a couple of days and find fault with the way their kids were being raised. Arty used to do the same thing.

Sal takes off the headphones and smiles. Puts the CDs and the player into one of the pockets of the greatcoat. It feels okay now, for him not to say anything. Just as it feels okay for Betty to wait. Wait for the answer that never comes. For Sal to tell her just one thing about himself. It could be anything. Not the thing she wants most to know – wanted to know from the very first time she saw him. Not that. Betty's pretty sure it must be that way for all women. They must all have met at least one man in their lives that it happened with. This same thing. Wanting to know that one thing. The one thing every woman wants to know about a man. The thing she can never find out. She doesn't even know what it is. Only that it has something to do with the boy in him. With the part of him that's small. Fragile. Childlike. Or maybe it's just me, thinks Betty. Maybe it's just because that's the thing I could never manage to see in my own son. It's true she was never able to find the child inside Tony. Even when he was a child.

But it's different with Sal. Betty can see that it's there, waiting to get out. This thing that has to do with smallness. It's what makes him different from other men. The fact that he listens from a place different than most men. The fact that Sal can make himself so small in the world makes him bigger than everyone else. He sees. He hears. He listens. And this gives him an inner bigness. Betty would like to travel there, to that place. Where he lives. Inside. The constant vulnerability of that. The funny thing is that he never says anything back to her, and yet, the times she talks to him are more like conversations than anything else in her experience. And that's only because he listens. Really listens. Sal can make himself small enough to do that. Take himself to a place not built out of a need for acknowledgement. Affirmation. A place inside himself that Betty has only glimpsed now and then when she looks deep into his moist eyes, into the silent garden of his own inner dignity. Sees there the thing he carries around with him always, the bold beauty of his quiet humility. How does a man get to a place like that, she wonders. What does it cost him? What must he sacrifice to reap the reward of such a graceful liberation?

They put Tony away for a year this time. Up at the penitentiary in Stony Mountain. Just as well. She knew it was coming, but it still hurt. For a mother to see her boy taken to a place like that. It hurt. At the trial, it was clear he was going to jail. Betty could tell as soon as she sat down in the courtroom that everyone had had enough. All of them. The judge, the police, the lawyers, the social workers, the psychologists, the probation officers. The girlfriend excited by it all. There was always a girlfriend. Some skinny little thing with tits and hair and attitude. They're always the same. Horny to fuck him because he's bad. This time it was Ginny, who sat next to Betty on the hard wooden bench, twitching in her tight little blue jeans, cracking her gum. The time before that it was Angie. Tony got off with probation that time, and Betty saw them going at it on the seat of the pickup truck out in the parking lot not ten minutes later. But not this time. This time they took him straight out and Arty had to drive Ginny home in the pickup truck. The judge sentenced him to a year in minimum security. So now on Sundays there's Betty, sitting with him outside the bungalow he shares with some of the other inmates. Arty waits in the car. The place isn't too bad, really. Nicer than what she and Arty have in some ways. They don't have a picnic table under the trees to sit on, for one thing.

Three motorcycles rumble noisily into the parking lot. Betty and Sal watch them through the window. Two men and a woman, all of them wearing black leather and heavy silver chains, get off their bikes, start slowly for the diner through the dusk. When Betty sees that it's Grace and her two friends she thinks about running to lock the door and putting up the Closed sign, but it's too early for that and besides, there's still Hank and Henry.

After the three of them have walked in through the door and sat down in the first booth, Betty gets up and brings over some menus and a pot of coffee.

"Hi, Betty," says Eddy. "How's business?" He pulls the elastic off his ponytail and lets his hair fall across his face. Carl rubs his short beard while he looks over the menu. Eddy spots Sal and nudges Carl. "Get a load of him."

"I gotta get me a coat like that," says Carl.

"We were just in the neighbourhood," says Grace. She grins up at Betty, smacks her gum. "Thought we'd stop in and say hi."

"We just came from Stony," says Carl. "Saw Tony."

"Tony up at Stony," says Eddy. "Hey, you're a poet, Carl. A goddamn fucking poet."

"He wasn't too friendly," says Grace. She's looking hard at Betty. "Thinks maybe he got a raw deal. Took the fall for the others."

"What others?" says Betty.

Grace just looks up at her and grins.

"What can I get you?" says Betty. "We're just getting ready to close."

"I'm so hungry I could eat the ass out of a rhinoceros," says Carl.

"What's good?" says Eddy.

"What do you mean, what's good?" says Grace. "It's all good. Right Betty?"

waiting for elvis

When they've placed their orders Betty turns to head for the kitchen and hears Eddy say, "Nice tits."

"You could stick one in each ear and listen to yourself go off," says Carl.

"I'd nibble a penis out of her shit," says Eddy.

"I'd eat it," says Carl.

"Listen to the two of you," says Grace. "You would want to fuck something that old?"

"She's not old," says Eddy.

"She's ripe," says Carl.

Sal can hear all of it. Is careful not to let them think he hears. Feels something growing inside him. Something he is afraid of.

Betty takes the order and heads for the kitchen. She turns, looks quickly over at Sal in a way that tells him to stay right there, that everything is fine, then goes in back to fix their order.

The three of them are talking loudly now, lighting cigarettes, passing a bottle around, but the whole time Grace is staring over at Sal. Once in a while she says something in a loud voice to one of the others. Laughs. Sal thinks her laugh is ugly. The kind you'd hear from someone who just hurt you and liked it. Sal watches her drink. The way she tips back the bottle with her eyes still on him reminds him of Harry. She tips the bottle down and coughs like mud is coming up in her throat, puts a hand up to whisper something into the ear of the man with the ponytail and gets up out of the booth.

Sal tries to make himself small, the way he's learned how to do. But somehow he already knows it isn't going to work on her. He can feel her coming for him. She knows, he thinks. She sees. Just like Harry used to. No hiding from people like that. Grace stops at the booth, stands there, hands on her shiny leather hips, staring down at him. Sal looks down into his coffee cup for a long time, but when he can't stand it any longer lifts his head and sees her grinning down at him.

"Hey, big fella," she says. "Mind if I sit down for a minute?"

She slips into the booth across from him, pulls out a cigarette and lights it with a big black lighter that clicks when she opens

waiting for elvis

it and sends up a huge flame. She sticks the cigarette deep into the flame and sucks it into life, puts her elbows up on the table and runs a filthy hand through her thick, matted hair while she blows smoke across at Sal. Sal wonders if she cuts it with a pair of dull scissors like he does his own. The smell of her is strong – a mixture of sweat and dirt and semen and leather. The way she stares across the booth at him is the way Harry used to do across the kitchen table. Like he was figuring something out. A way to get something done.

She leans back in the booth now, cigarette dangling from her lips. "Warm in here," she says, and pulls down the zipper on her black leather jacket. The jacket opens, and Sal can see she's not wearing anything underneath. Her breasts become more and more exposed as she wiggles from side to side, nestling into the booth. The whole time she's staring across the booth at Sal.

She pulls the cigarette from her mouth, a smile on her lips. Looks down at her own cleavage. Blows smoke into it. "You like what you see?" She lifts a black, silver-studded boot up onto the table. "You like my boots?" Her uneven smile is made of sharp yellow teeth. Too many for her mouth. Too big. "Maybe you want to take them off for me?" She arches her back and turns around to look over at the men sitting in the booth, drinking. Punching each other's leather jackets. Throwing their heads back. Laughing. Then she turns back to Sal. Leans forward.

"Say," she says. "You sure are a strapping fella. Even with that big ugly coat on I can see you're a man underneath there. Why don't you take that coat off, honey. Let me get a better look at you."

Sal still has the coffee cup clutched in his grip, but now she's playing one of her fingers along the back of his hand, running it up and down as she talks to him.

"Those are some big hands you got there, sonny boy. You know what they say about a man with big hands, don't you?"

Sal is staring into her mouth now, into the canine sharpness of her yellow eye teeth. They make him think of Little Elvis when he grinned over at him from the median.

waiting for elvis

"Are you going to talk to me?" she says.

Sal's mind is running in a thousand different directions to try and find a way out, like when he's running through the chains and doors and bumpers and windshields all hung up under the pines. All he can think about is Momma sitting on Harry's knee with her blouse open and Harry with a clothespin in one hand and the other around her neck.

Grace leans farther forward until the rounded bottoms of her pale and pendulous breasts brush lightly across the shiny Formica of the table. "Damn hangovers make me horny, you know? Always do. Make me want to fuck anything that moves." Her breath is a foul mixture of smoke and shit. "I already fucked them two," she says, nodding over her shoulder, "but to tell you the truth between the both of them they didn't even begin to scratch my itch, if you know what I mean. I like it rough. Especially with a hangover. I don't mean a little slushy stroke or two. I mean a knock-down, drag-out, pump and grind slap and tumble screaming scratching fuck from hell." She shakes her head back and forth quickly. Bits of dandruff flutter down to the table. "So what do you say, big boy? Think you could do that for me? Fuck me like that? Fuck me unconscious? Fuck me into tomorrow?"

When Sal doesn't answer, doesn't move except to look down into his coffee cup, Grace's tone suddenly changes. "Jesus Christ," she spits, "what the hell is all that shit you got in there anyway?" Since Betty gave him the coat Sal has managed to fill every available pocket with as much as it will hold. Grace reaches across the table and sinks her hand into one of the breast pockets, pulls out a fistful, uncurls her fingers. An assortment of small nuts and bolts, washers and screws clatter onto the table, some of them bouncing over the edge and down onto the floor. She reaches out again, into another pocket, and this time a spool of thread, a small plastic box, a few stones and bits of glass fall to the table. The last thing to leave her hand is a tiny battery that rolls over the edge and onto the floor. She finds an inside pocket and pulls out a piece of cloth that unravels and sends a heavy rusted railroad spike clunking onto the table.

waiting for elvis

Betty's out from the back now with a tray full of fries and burgers and milkshakes. She looks over at Sal, sees Grace sitting across from him, the table between them littered with items from his coat. She hurries over to the booth and Grace sits back, zips up her leather jacket a little. Something about the pasty whiteness of the tops of her breasts reminds Betty of the woman in the porno movie Arty accidentally left between the couch cushions the other night. He does that from time to time and for some reason Betty always sticks it in the machine and takes a quick look. They're all the same. Men with big cocks fucking women with big tits. No imagination. In this one the naked woman had breasts so enormous that they seemed not to belong to her, but to have been borrowed from another, much larger, much bigger woman. The woman was down on all fours, sucking a man who knelt on the lawn in front of her, and being fucked from behind by another kneeling man. The men both had grotesque, misshapen cocks, bent and semi-erect. The woman's breasts were so large and flabby they hung down to the ground like a cow's udders, nipples rubbing over the blades of green grass. When the man fucking her from behind increased his pumping action they began to rock back and forth until her breasts were swinging wildly, crazily, like two enormous water-filled sacks, slapping against the thighs of the man kneeling in front of her, slapping her own thighs going the other way. Betty thought it was just about the most repulsive thing she'd ever seen. She has an overpowering sense that Grace is the woman from the video. She has the same look of vulgar sexuality about her that fires Betty's anger. Grace squirms a little in her seat, grins defiantly up at Betty.

"About time, honey. A gal could starve to death in here."

"What do you think you're doing?"

"What do you mean? What does it look like I'm doing? I'm talking to handsome over here."

Betty can see the desperation in Sal's eyes. Knows he's ready to bolt out the door if only he could move.

"Get out of there."

"What are you, the fucking police?"

"What did you do?"

"Why? He your boyfriend or something?"

"I told you to get out of there."

"Jesus, Betty, you gotta learn to lighten up. You're starting to get on my nerves."

"You think this is a joke?"

"You tell me."

"I asked you a question."

"Well, how about I give you an answer. None of your fucking business, cunt. How's that?"

Betty slams the tray down onto the counter. "Get out. Out of my diner."

Hank and Henry have turned to see what's going on, and Eddy and Carl are on their way over.

"Hey, Grace," says Eddy. "What's up? Are you giving these nice folks a hard time?" He lifts a french fry off the tray and chews at it.

"Get out," says Betty. "All of you. Before I call the police."

"Hey wait a minute," says Carl. "We just got our order."

"Yea, Betty," says Grace. "We haven't eaten yet."

"And you're not going to. Not in here anyway. Take it with you. Take it and get out."

Grace slides slowly out of the booth, picks up a burger from the tray, unwraps it with her filthy hands and bites into it, all without ever taking her eyes off Betty. She chews slowly, deliberately, then spits it onto the floor. "This food tastes like shit." She punches her hand down on the tray and it clatters to the floor.

"You fucking bitch," says Betty, but before she can move Grace shoots out a hand and grabs Betty by the scruff of the neck with fierce strength, holds her there while she picks up the railroad spike from the table. She tests its weight in the palm of her hand and smiles at Betty, a cold smile of triumph Sal has seen before, seen it on Harry after he figured a new way to hurt him. Grace makes a fist, the spike wrapped inside it like a dagger.

But now the two truckers are up out of their seats and come striding over. "Okay boys and girls," says Hank. "Playtime's over." He wraps his huge fingers around Grace's wrist, holds it there.

Henry puts a hand on Eddy's shoulder and another on Carl's. "Time to get back on your trikes and ride, boys," he says.

They turn and look up at him. Take his measure. See how big he is.

"Come on, Grace," says Eddy. "What do you say we get out of this fuckin' dump?"

"Sure," says Grace. Tears herself out of Hank's grip. "Catch you later . . . Betty. Oh, and by the way," she straightens out her jacket, "make sure you tell Tony we came by."

The three of them turn, walk out through the door into the parking lot. Outside, they kick their bikes into life and ride off, spitting gravel.

"What the hell was that about?" says Hank.

"Nothing," says Betty. "Nothing at all. Sit down, boys. I'll get you some more coffee. And a cinnamon bun on me."

"What about your buddy here," says Henry. "He okay?"

"Yea," says Hank. "He looks a little pale."

"He's fine," says Betty. "Thanks."

"You know, Betty," says Hank, "you wouldn't have this kind of trouble if you didn't let him come around here so much."

"That so? Well if it becomes any of your business, I'll let you know."

"Jesus, Betty, take it easy," says Henry.

"I could have handled that bunch alright. I can look after my own place."

"Alright, alright," says Hank. The two men head back to their booth. Betty can hear them mumbling to each other. She puts a hand on Sal's shoulder.

"You okay?" she asks.

Sal clutches at his coffee cup. It glows. It burns.

chapter ten

"Alright, that's it," says Arty. He's talking to Betty while she changes the filter in the coffee machine. He leans in close to her now so the customers won't hear. "That's the last time that crazy son of a bitch comes in here." He's just now heard about what happened while he was out bowling the night before. Hank came in and Betty watched him spill the whole thing inside of a minute, sitting across from Arty in one of the booths. Betty could see from the way he was gesturing with his hands that in Hank's version they walked into the place just in time to keep Betty from getting knifed by a biker whore and a couple of her greasy fuck-buddies. How it was that smelly drifter Betty was always mollycoddling that seemed to be the cause of all the trouble. Something like that. So now Arty's come over to give her an earful.

Betty lifts the lid off the top of the coffee machine and pours in the water like she didn't hear a word he said.

"Are you listening to me?" says Arty. "I'm telling you he's not coming in here any more. I won't have it. All he does is cause trouble."

Finally she looks over at him. "It was that bitch who started it," she says, and puts the empty pot down underneath just as the hot coffee begins to run out in a smooth black column. "One of Tony's so-called friends. The new ones he made after you gave him that motorcycle. She practically rubbed her tits in his face."

"He's not coming through that door again."

"Sal didn't do anything wrong, Arty."

"I've tried to meet you halfway on this, Betty. I really have. But this has gone far enough."

"He was just sitting there minding his own business."

"It's always like that. Him minding his own business but cutting into mine."

"So that's what this is about."

"Goddammit, Betty, you know he's bad for business, and Hank says there could have been real trouble if they hadn't stepped in when they did. Who knows what the hell might have happened?"

"Hank likes to play himself up as a big hero. It was nothing I couldn't have taken care of myself."

"That's not the way he tells it."

"Sal wouldn't have let them do anything to me. I know he wouldn't."

"Hank says Sal didn't so much as lift one goddamn finger to help you."

"He didn't have to. I told you. Nothing happened."

"Doesn't matter. All I know is he's not good for the place, Betty. Truckers don't like him any more than I do. Only reason they put up with him being in here all the time is on account of you."

"Jesus, Arty, he doesn't spend more than a couple of hours a week in here."

"Did you ever stop to think how it looks, Betty? How it reflects on me? You taking such an interest in a drifter like him?"

"It always comes back to you somehow, doesn't it? It's always your pony getting whipped. Look, all I do is talk to him. That's all I do. Where's the harm in that?"

"That's another thing. That crazy bastard hasn't said a single word since he came in here."

"You don't get it, do you?"

"Oh I get it, alright."

"No, I don't think you do. We've got a chance to help somebody here, Arty. To do some good for someone. Someone who really needs it."

"Needs it? What about me?"

"Here we go again."

"How come you always do that?"

"What's that supposed to mean?"

"This isn't the first time. That's what I mean. You get yourself all bent out of shape over someone like that."

"Like what?"

"Goddammit, Betty, you know what I mean. It was the same with that hooker in Thunder Bay."

"Jesus, Arty, that was six years ago."

"It's the same thing. Don't you see? The same thing all over again. Sometimes you just don't know when to leave a thing alone."

The trip to Thunder Bay was about the only time the two of them had taken a little bit of a holiday in years. And even then they were going to pick up restaurant supplies from the wholesaler to take back with them. There were a couple of decent motels at the south end of town but Arty had insisted on staying in a place downtown where it was cheaper.

"That's the beauty," he'd said. "Same thing for half the price. A bed and a bath is all you need."

So it wasn't what Betty would have called a real holiday. Still, they'd gone out for a nice meal and they were walking back to the hotel when Betty saw a woman in the alleyway, slumped up against the brick wall between the hotel and the building next door. She wanted to look in on her, see if she was alright.

"That's nothing but a doped-up hooker," said Arty. "Leave her."

Betty looked at him when he said this, the way she'd looked at him so many times before. The look said that he had no business dismissing people so easily. Betty stepped into the alley, bent down and asked the woman if she was alright.

"Get the fuck away from me," she slurred, the words all tied up in booze and terror and despair. She looked up at Betty. "Cunt." Then at Arty. "Son of a bitch."

"Jesus," said Arty. "Leave her, Betty. She's probably a whore. A junkie. Or both."

But Betty stayed next to her and then got her up and sitting against the wall. Even in the dim light it was easy to see that she had been beaten up. "Do you need a doctor?" said Betty.

"Doctor," the woman said to her. She looked up at Arty. "She wants to know if I need a fuckin' doctor." Then she turned back to Betty. "You're not gonna let him fuck me, are you?"

"Oh, man," said Arty. "Let's go. She's gonna be alright."

"Who did this to you?"

"What the fuck do you care?"

"Where do you live?" said Betty. "We'll take you home. Come on, Arty. Help me get her up."

"I don't want to go home," said the woman. "I want to stay right here. The cops'll find me soon enough. They always do." But it was cold that night and this woman was wearing only a short skirt and a skimpy little blouse that was torn. Now that she was up Betty could see what a small woman she really was. Petite. She was tiny and that made Betty want to help her just that much more. To be tiny in the world. Like Sal. Not that he was a small man. But Betty didn't mean it that way. She meant about the inside of a person. That was something special. To make yourself small. To let yourself become small. Feel small. Sal knew how to do that and somehow that made him terribly important. More important than somebody big and imposing. To be small. That was important. To let the world be so big around you. So big. You could see it better that way.

They got her out onto the sidewalk. The thing Betty has remembered all these years is how ridiculous that little skirt looked on the woman, there on the sidewalk, all shifted sideways and wrinkled up the way it was. Like it didn't belong on her body – on any woman's body.

"That way," said the woman. She pointed and they walked for a couple of blocks. "There," she said, and indicated a run-down building across the street. They staggered the drunken woman up an outside flight of stairs to a chipped and dirty door and knocked. A man opened it up. He was bare chested and rubbed his beer belly while he looked them over.

Betty hated him instantly. Hated the way he looked. She'd told Arty long ago that if he ever allowed himself to grow a stomach like that she'd divorce him. She meant it. She doesn't know why she hates that so much, but it has something to do with back when she was still Elizabeth and a blanket and grass and trees and her father's bare chest. It was a long time ago. They were on a picnic – she and her father and mother. Her father had taken his shirt off. It was very hot. He was talking to Betty's mother.

"A man with a flat stomach," he said, "is a man with a future." There were a lot of other men around and some of them had their shirts off just like her father, but most of them had bellies – some that bulged right out over their belts. The irony was that most of these pot-bellied men would be walking around long after her father was dead and buried. Betty was looking at his tanned and sleek upper torso. He had a good chest, and his stomach, with only a little hair on it, was flatter than any of the other men's. He was lying down on a blanket they were all sharing under a large shade tree. His head rested in her mother's lap. He had a bottle of beer in one hand. The other was rubbing lightly – Betty can still remember how lightly – across the downy hair on his smooth stomach.

"You can't let a thing like that get out of hand. Before you know it that thing starts to grow and then one day it's just hanging there and you look down and you can't see your own dick."

"Please, George," said her mother. "Elizabeth."

"What kind of man are you then? No kind. You might as well just say to the world, 'look at me, all I do is eat and shit.' That's what you're saying. There's a kind of giving up in that."

waiting for elvis

Standing there in the decrepit doorway of the rundown apartment building, looking at that man's hairy and enormous beer belly, Betty wanted it all to be right again. Wanted this man to be dead. Her father to be alive.

"What the fuck are you doing back here," the man said to the woman, "you fuckin' cunt."

"He's drunk," says Arty. "Leave her and let's go."

"Who you callin' drunk mister?" The man was looking at Arty now, swaying from side to side.

"Can we get out of here before this guy takes a swing at me?" said Arty.

"She can freeze to death for all I care. She's nothing but a gutter slut anyway. Gutter's the place for her. And she's a thief. Drunken bitch stole my booze and took off with it."

"It's alright," said the woman. Pulling herself in through the doorway. "Thank you," she said to Betty. She meant it. "I'll be alright. Really. Thanks."

Back at the hotel Arty wasn't ready to let it go. He got a beer of his own out of the cooler, the one they'd brought up with them so they could save money on food and drinks. "What in the hell do you want to go and get messed up with people like that for? No good reason I can think of. You're just asking for trouble."

"No good reason," Betty repeated the words back at him. "You honestly can't think of one."

"You tell me," said Arty. But before Betty could even begin to try and formulate a meaningful answer, he added, "You think someone's gonna do the same for you someday. Is that it? Well, I got news for you. The world doesn't work that way. Never has. Never will. People don't give a damn about each other. Not about you or me or anybody. What you did won't change that. You can't change a thing like that."

"So the best thing is to do nothing. Is that what I should have done?" The truth was that the whole time she was doing it Betty never once stopped to ask herself why. But she knew she'd do it again. Arty did, too.

waiting for elvis

But she also knows it's different with Sal. Deeper. More important. She takes out the fresh pot and pours two steaming cups of coffee.

"Take those," she says to Arty. "People are waiting."

"Let them wait," says Arty. "We gotta settle this."

"There's nothing to settle."

"The hell there isn't. You get yourself all bent out of shape over a complete stranger, but when it comes to your own goddamn son . . ." When he sees the look on Betty's face he knows he's crossed a line. Entered dangerous and unfamiliar territory. He's frozen now, the coffee cups steaming in his hands.

The long silence between them is broken by Betty's quiet, even voice.

"That was a damn dirty thing to say to me, Arty."

"Well, goddammit, Betty, somebody had to say it." Arty's bluffing now. He can hear it in his own voice. But there's no turning back. "We can't just let things go on like this."

"We've done talking."

"You have to tell him."

"Tell who?"

"That drifter."

"Tell him what?"

"You know damn well what. I'll call the cops if he comes in here again."

Betty takes the cups out of his hands and walks away.

"I will," Arty says a little louder than he wanted to. Sees Hank looking over at them and heads for the back to check on the grill.

All the rest of that afternoon, while she's pouring cups of coffee and serving up cinnamon buns, Betty can't stop thinking about what will happen the next time Sal comes around. What Arty might do. What she might do. He doesn't get it about Sal the same way he never did about his own son. It always took something drastic to shake him into reality. And even then it never lasted. The first time it really hit him he was back from a long haul and getting cleaned up. Tony was only five, standing on a chair next to the sink, watching his father shave. Arty always used a straight razor back then. Still does. Stopped for a couple of weeks after what happened but then went right back to it.

"Can I see?" said Tony.

"See what?" said Arty.

"That."

"You mean this?" Arty held out the straight razor. "That's sharp," he said. "Dangerous. When you're older."

Arty went back to shaving his neck and Tony made a grab for the razor.

"Jesus Christ," said Arty, turning to keep the razor out of Tony's reach while Betty went to grab him off the stool.

"No," said Arty. "It's alright. Here," he said to Tony. "Put your hand on the back of mine. We'll do it together." He took Tony's little hand and placed it carefully on the back of his. Tony looked over at Betty, and then instead of moving his hand up and down along with Arty's like he was supposed to he yanked it sideways.

"Son of a bitch!" said Arty. Put his other hand where the razor had sliced his neck open. Blood poured out between the fingers. The thing Betty will never forget is the look on his face. Pale with fear, but not for his wound. He was looking over at Tony, and seeing for the first time what Betty had seen before. There was Tony, still standing on the stool, grinning up at his father like he'd just done something he was proud of.

Then there was the time he walked in on the two of them in bed one night. Arty was just spending himself in that same urgent way he did after a long road trip when the door opened quickly and Tony stepped in, flipped the switch to turn on the light that Arty always wanted off, and stood there watching Arty try to stop himself in mid-thrust. Betty looked over at him, her legs open, hands up on Arty's back. Tony was just standing there with his small arms folded. The thing Betty will always remember is the complete lack of surprise on his face. No sense of wonder or awe or fear. No confusion or even shame. None of those things. In its place was that same smile. The one no six-year-old had any business wearing. A smile that said he was thinking what no six-year-old boy should be thinking about.

It was like that from the very beginning. All the things that should have delighted a boy his age failed to do so. The way he didn't want to play with any of the toys they bought him. The way he only wanted to play with other children when there were no adults around. Always that undercurrent of something else going on in his mind. A certain restless dissatisfaction. It never seemed to Betty that there was a child inside that body. Never the look of a child in those eyes.

It's getting on to closing time when Betty hears something in the kitchen. She knows Arty went back there to scoop some old shortening out of the deep fryer and into a pail to cool overnight, but then the big stainless steel ladle clanks down onto the floor and a deep, intense groan comes through the service window, a little like the way he sounds when he's spending himself inside her, except that this is all wrong somehow. She drops the coffee pot and runs in through the back to find Arty slumped against the fryer, clutching at his chest. His other hand is submerged in the smoking oil, broiling like an oversized french fry.

"Dammit," she shouts loud enough for the rest of the diner to hear, rushes over to him. She tries to lift his arm out of the hot oil, splatters some on her own body, yells out to the front, "In here. Goddammit, somebody help me." Harvey runs in through the doors and together they get Arty's arm free and lower him to the tile floor, slick now with oil.

Another trucker comes running in. "Jesus Christ," he says, bends down on one knee over Arty and helps Harvey turn him over on his back.

"Call an ambulance," Betty says, looking up. "Hurry."

She kneels over Arty, listens to his breathing come in small sharp inhalations, punctuated by a rasping gurgle deep in his lungs. His eyes open. Close again. He moans strangely. Deeply.

"It's alright." Betty leans close. "Don't try to move. The ambulance is on its way. You have to lay still. Stay quiet. Just breathe, Arty."

Somebody pulls a towel off the rack and puts it under Arty's head. Betty cradles his burned arm in her lap. It feels so heavy. His arm. So heavy. The skin up to the elbow is boiled and white, like a raw donut. The back of the hand is peeled away exposing raw flesh. There's no blood.

The arm that has been clutching at his chest reaches out to her, grabs her forearm where the oil spilled on it, squeezes until Betty wants to scream in pain. Then Arty's whole body stiffens, rigid now, eyes open, pupils like dark saucers, mouth open, and Betty hears what she knows is the long gasp of her husband's last breath.

"I don't know what to do," she says. She looks up at the truckers gathered around. "Does anybody know what to do?"

Even before the ambulance arrives Betty, in spite of herself, feels the dull edge of resignation cutting across her chest, then stabbing into her stomach. The subtle giving in to the negative space she watched Arty disappear into. The place where three dimensions become two. The flat, dull world of the dead.

chapter eleven

WHEN BETTY PULLS UP TO THE DETENTION CENTRE Tony's already waiting outside for her on the other side of the gate, one sleek-booted foot crossed over in front of the other, leaning against the large brick building, cigarette dangling from his lip. She's here to pick him up for the funeral. They've agreed to release him into her custody. She pulls up to a stop, looks out through the windshield at her son. He's smoking the cigarette with the same urgency to consume that he has for everything else. Sucking hard, biting down on the filter, blowing smoke like it was poison. Nothing about his demeanour gives the slightest indication that he's going anywhere special. Certainly not to his father's funeral. It was a massive heart attack that killed Arty, just like she always knew it would be. Knew, just like she knew what was coming with Tony and with her mother, and – she understands now – just like she knew even when it was her father all the way back when she was still Elizabeth. But she wasn't ready then and she isn't now.

There's a Closed sign on the diner, but only for today. It'll be business as usual tomorrow. A few of the truckers are bound to show up for the funeral, and the rest will manage for a day without her. She's not sure why she's kept the diner open. The regulars think it's on account of what Arty would have wanted and she goes along with it, but she knows that's not really it. It has a lot more to do with her fear. With being afraid of what might happen if Sal came around and she wasn't there. It would be easy to let that make her feel like she was being disloyal to Arty somehow, but she's not going to allow it. She's tired of feeling that way about everything. She's had enough of guilt. It's a feeling she doesn't trust anymore. What good has it ever done her? It's always been someone else who got the benefit from it. Why should she allow it to come so easily, so conveniently, when it never changes anything? Who is it really for?

The guard on duty steps over to her side of the car while Tony gets in and hands her a clipboard. Tony's slicked-back hair is long and unkempt, the stubble of a scruffy beard impertinent and uneven on his face. That face with the same twisted features. He's wearing a black T-shirt and torn blue jeans pulled over a pair of scuffed boots.

The guard leans into the window. "He has to be back by nine," he says. Stares into Betty's blouse. Looks over at Tony. "You know that."

"I know," says Betty.

"Just so you know," says the guard. He's looking right at Tony.

"I'll tell you what I know," says Tony, leering back at the guard. "One less day in this shithole. That's what I know."

After Betty signs and they're back out on the highway she says, "We're stopping at the house. You can get cleaned up and there's a suit for you to wear."

"I'm not wearing any goddamn suit."

"And don't forget to shave."

"I'm not wearing any fucking suit and I'm goddamn well not shaving."

"And the next swear word that comes out of your mouth we're turning right around and going back."

"Bullshit we are. I got a day pass." He sticks an arm out the window, yells out, "I'm a free man."

"Not if I say you aren't."

"You signed the paper. It's a done deal."

"There's nothing on that paper that says I can't take you back any time I like." She sees the doubt begin in his eyes.

"I don't think so."

"Try me. You're out on my say so. And I say you'll do what you're told or go back."

"Jesus Christ." He pounds the dashboard with one fist, reaches for the cigarettes in his pocket with the other.

"No smoking in the car. You can have one later. There'll be time."

"Son of a bitch."

Betty slams on the brakes.

"Alright, alright. Sorry. Just drive." He cowers into a sulk, leans against the far door and stays there for the rest of the trip into town while Betty can only drive and wonder how it's possible for her to have raised a son who turned out this way. She thinks about saying it right out loud to his face, but she knows it wouldn't do any good. Besides, she knows the answer. The answer is that she didn't raise him to turn out this way at all. What mother ever did? It was never like that. From the very beginning something else was at work. Something out of her hands. Out of Arty's hands. Out of everyone's.

At the funeral Tony's behaviour is the same as it has always been at every other ceremony he's ever attended. Everything about his presence has a kind of tightness to it, bound up in circles and twists of dissatisfaction. In everything he says and does there is a kind of urgency, of need to get on to the next thing and spoil it. To corrode the place with the acid of his petty need.

Later, while people gather back at the house, he fails to show even one ounce of sensitivity to the situation. To Betty. No arm around her shoulder. No words of comfort. These things are not in his repertoire. No sudden burst of tears that he's been holding back. No revelation about how he will turn his life around now, for the sake of his father. The entire event is lost on him, as the entire sequence of his pitiful life has been. He laughs at all the wrong times, disdainfully, in a way that is meant to provoke. Disturb. He stares back at people who turn to give him a look. The same cold stare. Meant to belittle. Challenge. Weaken. His entire body dares anyone to say something, do something. So he can fly into a rage.

They make the trip back to the prison in silence. Betty finds herself thinking about her own father's funeral, how she stood with her favourite doll in one hand, holding her mother's hand with the other, stared into the coffin. How her mother was not looking down at her, or into the coffin, but up, instead, at the vaulted ceiling of the church, as if she were searching intently there for some kind of answer. What was it her mother was looking for so desperately that day? God? Someone to blame? Some way to make sense of it all?

Back at the diner Betty is just as glad for the dull, bludgeoning routine of it all. The predictable sameness of the truckers and their needs. They are a little more silent, a little more respectful, but she knows that will soon change. Everything is up for grabs now as far as they're concerned. Soon some of them will start making suggestive remarks they wouldn't have made before. The line that was always there – the one they stopped at when they tried to flirt with her – will be a little easier to cross. They will risk more now. Start to try and take small liberties when they think they can get away with it. But she's ready for it. It's nothing she can't handle.

Running the place without Arty hasn't been as hard as she thought. She's been doing the work of both of them, but also changed things around a little. The regulars fetch their own coffee now, and cutlery if they have to. Shout their orders in through the back when she's too busy to come out and take them. Missing Arty is something different, though. Not at all what Betty thought it would be. She didn't expect it to hurt this much. But the physicality of it surprises her. Not in the way she would miss an absent lover, though. Not like that. That would be in her stomach. This is higher up. A mild humming in her chest. The negative space of her longing is more about the routine of him. She doesn't want to admit it to herself but the truth is a lot of it is the way the days of her life revolved around her dissatisfaction with him. The absence of it tugging at her insides. The field of its steady, constant gravity gone. The place where her discontent used to dwell no longer there for her to orbit. In its place a certain odd and discomfiting sense of increasing weightlessness.

Part of what Betty feels about losing Arty has to do with simple comfort. With no longer being able to look out at life through the filtered lens of his constant presence. The sudden unfamiliarity of life without someone else at the breakfast table, on the couch in front of the television, snoring on the far side of the bed. It's been a month and she has yet to venture over there – to his side of the bed. She could sleep there if she felt like it. She could choose to occupy that space. Try it out. But even her side of the mattress feels different now. The whole bed feels lighter. There's a certain absence of weight.

Even silly things like all the annoying night noises he made. His farting. Snoring. Sighing. Scratching. Belching. Tossing. Grunting. All gone. Silence. Only the sound of her own breathing now. All through the night. Then the foggy, moody morning of coffee and breakfast all to herself. The barren quiet of that.

She finds herself attaching value where none existed before. To the comfort of the other's presence, however distant. Unseen. There's something to be said for just knowing that there's another human being somewhere in the house. There's something in that. Now, when she feels the need to say something out loud, there's no one to hear. It isn't about listening. It never was. Just someone to be there who could hear the words. It's not such a little thing. She can't imagine how Sal does it. His silence amazes her.

Some things don't feel the way they used to. Like her loneliness. She was always lonely. Only now it's changed form. It's become more immediate. More direct. More free-floating, to go with the lack of gravity. Darker, to go with the lack of light. At least, before, she and Arty could be isolated – one from the other. But now there's no one to take the edge off. Two people, each leaning against the unfulfilled wishes of the other. There was a certain reliability in that. A certain comfort in the failed expectations two people could have of each other.

To go from the known to the unknown. That's what's giving her this hollow chest. Making her muscles and bones ache. She finds herself leaning forward a lot. In her chair. Against the counter. The steering wheel. Leaning into something. The space where the familiar used to be. She feels a certain free-floating anger simmering away inside her. Mostly because of the fact that part of her insists on wanting things to be the way they were – just because they no longer can be. The nagging, insidious power of that. Sometimes it's merely the finality of a thing that makes it so compelling. It's the not having a choice.

Even her dreams are different. There have been a lot of dreams since it happened. This time it was Arty's face – huge, wrinkled and ominous, surrounded by smoke and fire – that appeared before her like some conjured special effect from *The Wizard Of Oz*. And then she was Dorothy and Toto was pulling the curtain and there was this lumpy little man pushing buttons and turning knobs. It was Arty. And Sal was in there somewhere, too, as the straw man. Or maybe it was the lion. And Tony was one of those awful flying monkeys. And Betty was little Judy Garland. Singing "Somewhere Over The Rainbow" against a stack of hay, then wading through a sea of colourfully dressed Munchkins, accepting their flowers and adulation, and then clicking her heels together and intoning, "There's no place like home. There's no place like home."

chapter twelve

"All I'm saying is what do you really know about the guy," says Harvey. He's sitting up at the counter, across from Betty, staring at the menu. He's been coming in a lot since Arty died – taken on an air of familiarity that Betty doesn't care for. As though he's entitled to more now.

"How much do I know about you?" says Betty. "About anybody? What do people really know about each other?"

"He's out there living like a wild animal, Betty. That's not right. You do that, pretty soon you start acting like one. I mean, look at him."

Sal is sitting at the far end of the diner in the same booth he always chooses. He came in this morning, early. Just after Betty got there to open up the place. He was cut up and bruised like other times, and he has that look in his eyes, that way of holding his head so you can only see into his eyes for a split second at a time. But even in those first few, brief glimpses Betty could see he'd been to that place again. The one she can only imagine. Saw that he was in the process of trying to make his way back, a little at a time, in such small careful steps. His entire being dangerously fragile. When she looked into his green eyes, it was through many layers of fluorescent and incandescent shards, the shattered fragments through which his soul still shines.

She ran to meet him. Took his great, wounded hands in hers, led him in through the door. She took his coat off and hung it on the rack. He let her. Took him right to the back and stripped him to the waist. Washed his wounds, cleaned them, soothed them. Later, she fed him soup and milk and tea. She would have taken out her breast and let him suckle it, if she'd had nourishment there for him. Comfort. She wanted to send him something good from her body. One living being to another. She understood, for the first time, that when he came back from one of these episodes, in many ways he needed to be born again. She wanted to offer herself to him. Accept his furtive glances of blank and uncomprehending wonder for what they were. The innocence of the newborn.

When he was cleaned up, she put fresh clothes on him – things she'd bought for Arty only a week before he died because he never bought clothes for himself. A pair of jeans and a plaid shirt. She'd brought them with her to the diner, ready for the next time Sal came in. Thought she might as well put them to good use even though they weren't quite the same size. Arty was bigger around the middle and smaller at the shoulders but she always got him a size too large because he liked loose-fitting clothes, so it was alright when Sal put them on. Then she bedded him down in the bunk at the back and watched him fall into a restless sleep. For a crazy instant she thought of leaving the Closed sign on the door and laying down next to him, but instead she got busy with the rest of her day and went out front to unlock the door just as the first trucker pulled his rig into the parking lot.

Sal spent the day on the bunk. Slept and slept and slept. The customers who came and went had no idea he was even there. Betty wouldn't have cared if they had. But now he's up, sitting in the same booth he always does. She's told him to wait there. No matter what. Wait for Betty to come and sit across from him.

Harvey's gone back to staring at the menu even though Betty is sure he must know it by heart. He always makes sure to ask for one, makes a big deal out of taking it from her when she hands it to him, makes sure his hand rubs against hers. She's going to tell him to get it himself the next time he does that.

"What's it going to be, Harvey? I got things to do." This much is true. It's always true now that Arty's gone, but what Betty is really thinking about is having some time alone with Sal. She wants Harvey gone so she can ask him. The thing she's decided not to put off any longer. The thing she couldn't have asked when Arty was still alive. But now, suddenly, it's okay. She wants to.

"I think I'll go for the chili today," he says. He always orders the chili. "Nobody makes chili like you do, Betty."

And when she does ask him, she will look for the answer in his eyes. There are only small, precious moments when Sal will allow her to look into them. As if he fears that by allowing someone to look too long, too deep, they might stare him out of existence. She senses that fear in him. That he can open the window to his soul only a crack. Or risk withering and dying right there, before her eyes. When she saw him hobbling across the parking lot, something oddly familiar happened to her body. Something she hadn't felt since she was pregnant with Tony – and never since. A surge of desire. Of deep connection. With Tony, it was about the chord, newly formed, stretched and folded between them. The chord through which she would send him so many good things. Fill him up with the best of herself. It was the happiest time of her life, being pregnant with Tony. It was only after he was born that all the trouble and disappointment began. The dark spiral of confusion, and inadequacy. Unexplainable. But when he was being formed she felt as wonderful as she could ever remember.

Betty heads for the back and Harvey keeps talking to her through the service window. Louder now.

"All I'm saying is you can't trust a guy like that," he says.

"There's plenty of people I don't trust," says Betty. "But he's not one of them."

"I'm just trying to look out for you is all."

"Thanks, Harvey, but I'm a big girl. I can look after myself."

"Isn't a woman on Earth that doesn't need some looking after."

"Or man either," Betty says.

The thing that surprised her most, seeing Sal after such a long absence, was how she wanted more than ever to plug herself in to him. Feed him energy. Life. Nourishment. To find some way to make him whole again. Rebuild him, piece by piece. To soften the wild, dispossessed look of him a little. Only a little. Not completely. Never completely. Something about the tumble of his dishevelled hair, the feel of his rough and scarred hands, the scratch of his whiskers.

He's in the booth now, his coat off, hanging on the rack where Betty first took it down and got him to try it on. She talked him into leaving it there instead of putting it back on again. He submitted with a silent grace, but there was a certain nakedness about it, as there always is – like he was allowing her to remove a layer of his skin. And this is exactly what she wants to do. Peel away the layers of him. Until she reaches the core. The centre. The place where he honestly and truly dwells.

It is a source of constant amazement to her that this silent and troubled man should bring so much happiness into her life. It doesn't make any sense. Maybe it's stronger now that Arty's gone. Something to do with the freedom. With mercy. There's a new sense of contentment this time. Of patience. It's enough now, to have him near. To care for him. About him. With him. The rest may come. It may not. A certain serenity has washed over her this time. It will all take time. It will start, as all the new chapters in her life have, with small, insignificant gestures of great importance. Things no one else would take notice of. Only she will know how important they are. What they truly mean.

She was looking out at him just now, sitting in the booth in his shirt sleeves. She knew he must be feeling a little naked. But in a minute she was going to come out and sit down across from him, face to face. Talk. As long as it takes.

Talking to Sal is an open ticket. And yet, in spite of that tremendous freedom, the strange thing is that she never chooses her words more carefully than when she speaks to him. The easy dismissal of mindless conversation – the kind she hears going on all through the diner day after day – is the very thing she takes great pains to avoid. Sal deserves much better than that. And so does she. It must never, never be about hearing the sound of her own voice. It would be so wrong to do that with Sal. A form of abuse. She must speak to him – always – as if it were perfectly reasonable and possible for him to answer. As if that were the very thing she was expecting. She must never allow herself to slip into the complacency of not needing an answer. Of not expecting one.

There's a certain patience in that, but it's not about waiting. Not about hours or minutes or days or weeks. It exists outside of time. Of space. She will help him to emerge, little by little, from under the shadow of his own suffering. And all the while, it will be her job to acknowledge its existence, however unseen, however unimagined. Simply to accept that something awful happened to him. Some terrible horrible thing he will never speak of. And even when the shadow of that is gone, the memory of it will remain. So strong that to say it can never be forgotten is to insult its power. To mock its very nature – this thing so imbedded in every fibre and tissue of his body.

So much about him is still raw. The aftermath of his affliction so fresh. The odour of his recent anguish still clearly detectable, giving the air around him an acidic taste. A certain intensity in each of his movements – every breath, touch of a tabletop, spoon, cup. The pain still so very close to the surface. And also the tenderness born of that pain. A softness not of comfort but fragility. The immense vulnerability of that. Pain transformed into grace. A sense of metamorphosis. Every molecule of his body cleansed. Purified. Sal as angel. Sal as priest. Spirit. Sal with a soul as white as pure light.

Betty understands that he can't bring himself to look back into her eyes too long, too deeply. Can't afford to let her – to let anyone – see all of that. Too much openness is dangerous. There is still too much capacity for further, greater suffering. And yet, there is the unmistakable capacity for wonder as well. The light of that shines through as brightly as anything. In spite of all the hurt behind them. But these are not the eyes of a madman. They do not burn that way. They do not smoulder. The incandescence there is like the glow of a white candle, bright with the possibility, the hope, of peace. Of serenity.

Betty doesn't want to know what happened. She doesn't want to understand it. This great secret that lies behind his silence. She merely wants to acknowledge it, this awful thing that takes him so far away. And help him to get back. Somehow to find a way to return to his humanity. Perhaps his silence is the very thing that allows him to maintain his sense of innocence. Of dignity. How else could he have managed to hold on to it? Perhaps, if he spoke, it would all burst into flame. Combust the windows of his soul. Burn them to ash. Turn them into dull and opaque cinders. And so he denies himself words. Because he must.

His freedom somehow lies in his wordless suffering. In the simple mercy she can offer because of it. Is it possible that words, by their very nature, would destroy all that mystery? That depth of connection? Sever the chord between them? When Sal finally gets born into the into the world of words again, will the act of speaking them ruin everything? She won't let that stop her. She will have to take that chance.

When Betty looks out from the back for a second to see why Harvey's gone so quiet she sees him sitting in the booth across from Sal, talking across the table at him. She leans out through the order window to try and make out what he's saying.

"All that shit you got in the pockets of that coat over there," she hears Harvey say, "picked up off the side of the road. That's what they say. Say you pick that stuff up out of the ditch. That true?"

Betty can see the discomfort building in Sal's eyes.

"Say you won't talk to anybody. Even though you know how. You got a place up there in the pines, too. That right? No electricity. No water. Guess you must have to take a shit in the woods like a goddamn smelly old bear, huh?" Harvey is laughing now, but in a hard kind of way, while Sal stares into his coffee cup.

"Sal. What kind of a name is that anyway, eh? That short for Sally or something? Sally. That's a girl's name."

There's an edge in Harvey's voice that tells Betty he's made up his mind about something. That he's not going to stop until he gets it.

"You like Betty, don't you? You talk to her I bet. Eh? Maybe you'd like to do more than just talk. Can't say I blame you. Eh? Isn't a man in this place hasn't thought about that. That what you got planned, Sally? Take over where Arty left off? Eh? You know what I think? I think you've been trying to fool people around here. Got everyone feeling sorry for you. Betty especially. Well I don't feel one damn bit sorry for you. You might be fooling everyone else around here but not me. I got a pretty good idea what you're up to. Had you figured right from the start. And now that Arty's out of the way, you figure you're gonna get what you came for. Well not while I have anything to say about it. If anybody's gonna wind that woman's watch it's gonna be me. Understand?"

Betty can hear everything Harvey's saying. Thinks maybe he wants it that way. Wants her to hear. She rushes out from the back with a white paper bag. Hurries over to the booth.

"Okay, Harvey, that's enough."

"Aw hell, Betty, I wasn't hurtin' him any. Just trying a little conversation, that's all."

"Leave him alone."

"You said yourself you think maybe he can talk. Right? Isn't that right, Sally?"

"Sal," says Betty as calmly as she can. "His name is Sal."

"Sure, whatever you say. No harm in trying to make a little conversation, is there? What about it, Betty? Talks to you sometimes, I bet. Don't he? But not to any of us. How come that is? Too good for us? That it?"

"I won't tell you again, Harvey."

"Look at him, Betty. Don't talk. Don't wash. Don't work. Just what the hell is he good for, anyway?" He looks up at Betty, then over at Sal. He reaches out and puts a hand on her hip. "Or maybe you can tell me." She slaps his hand off roughly.

"Here's your chili, Harvey," she says, holding out the white paper bag to him.

"What's that?"

"I made it to go."

"What for? I'm not going anywhere."

"That's where you're wrong." She pushes the bag into his chest. "On the house. A going-away present."

"Now wait a minute, Betty."

"Goodbye, Harvey."

"Christ, Betty. Take it easy. I didn't mean nothing."

"Sure you did."

"Now listen to me, Betty. Arty's gone and, goddammit, you need looking after. And he sure as hell isn't the man to do it. He's not even a man."

"Get out of here, Harvey," she says calmly. "Can you do that for me?"

"You got no business to treat me this way, Betty." Harvey slides out of the booth. Picks up the bag. "Alright. Have it your way." Then he looks over at Sal. "But you better just watch your step, pal. I got my eye on you." Harvey heads for the door, but just before he opens it he turns and says, "Arty wouldn't like this, Betty. He didn't like it then and he wouldn't like it now."

Betty only stands with her hands on her hips, waiting for him to leave.

"You're gonna be sorry about this one day, Betty. Real sorry."

Then he's out in the parking lot heading for his bus. After he's gone Betty sits down across from Sal, looks at him to see how he's doing. She doesn't want him shutting down. Not now.

And she makes up her mind then and there to make the request. The one she's been putting off. The one with a reply that doesn't require words. Just a simple act. She's been telling herself he's not ready, but she suddenly realizes it's been her that wasn't ready – until now. At first she wanted to try and get him thinking about the possibility of words again. Just one word. That's how she thought it would have to begin. With a single word. The right word to help them break through his silence. But now she understands that something else is needed.

She finds his green eyes. Tries to hold them.

"I need you to take me," she says.

His eyes drop down to the coffee cup between his hands, but only for a second, then come back up.

"I need you to show me," she says.

She leans forward, places a hand on his.

"Your place. In the woods. I want to see it."

She can feel him stiffen under her touch. See the hesitation in his eyes.

"Take me there. Please."

She gets up and slides out of the booth. Pulls the hand she is holding with her.

"I want to go right now."

She puts her hands together on his, tugs him out of the booth.

"I know it can't be far."

Now she's pulling him toward the door.

"It'll be alright. I promise. It'll be okay."

chapter thirteen

BETTY FOLLOWS SAL ALONG A PATH THAT SKIRTS THE edge of the forest, just far enough in so they won't be spotted from the road. She can see from the deer tracks here and there that it must be an animal trail. All that tonnage hurtling down the highway is close enough to tremble the spongy forest floor beneath her feet. The high-pitched howl of tires spinning over asphalt is a constant in her ears, along with the pungent taste of engine exhaust on her tongue like sour ash.

Sal moves before her, hunched over, his broad back bent. He understands about the way deer move through the forest – not like human creatures at all – not upright but down on all fours so they can slip under the low-hanging foliage and make the trail less noticeable. He's used to the constant bending to get under branches that a deer's back would just slide under, but for Betty it's like a long crouch until all she can think about is how much she wants to straighten up and walk erect again. Still, this way of moving makes it feel more like a furtive trek into a secret world, a journey to a forbidden place.

Then they make a sharp turn deeper into the woods and she can straighten up after they step into a small clearing. Betty stands for a moment, taking it all in: the clapboard shack, the

waiting for elvis

piles of different salvage collected from each day's journey along the side of the highway, the boards nailed up between the pines for a few pots and utensils to rest on. Boxes and crates stacked here and there against trees. When they were still out on the trail the whole thing had a sense of adventure to it, a thrill, but that's gone now. The place isn't what she imagined. She doesn't know why she should have expected anything else, though. She really had no business thinking it would be like something out of *The Swiss Family Robinson,* some romanticized version of a forest dwelling. There's not much to see, really, but she can't escape the guilt of her disappointment.

There's a haphazard ring of rocks near one end of the clearing for a fire, a little wood piled up next to it. A few ropes tied between the trees. The shack is as unappealing as the debris that surrounds it, as the noise of the highway still plainly audible in her ears. But when she turns to look back at Sal he tries to smile at her in that fragile way he has that tells her she must be careful. That she must treat this place as she has always treated him. With the same gentle consideration.

When she moves to the shack he follows her close, lets her pull back the door to look inside while he stands off to one side. She takes a step into the dim interior, makes out the small table, one battered chair pulled up to it, a clutter of cans and boxes and plastic bags on a clapboard shelf above it, a broken wooden rocking chair in one corner. There's nothing here of home. Of comfort or solace. Everything speaks of solitude. This has always been and ever will be a place of refuge and isolation. Of loneliness. There's a ruin about it. A wretchedness. And none of it is very pretty. She understands that this is a place no human would really want to inhabit, including Sal, that it was never meant to be the kind of place you would want to share with anyone else. What matters most is the need to respect the fact no one else has ever seen it. That he's never revealed it to anyone but her.

"There's no bed," she says. Turns to him, just outside. Looks at him through the doorway. Sees him shake his head.

"Where do you sleep?"

He beckons her back outside and they head across the clearing to where the hammock is strung up between the trunks of two tall pines. Betty walks up to it, tests the fabric with her fingers. Heavy. Like leather.

"You sleep here?"

She can almost walk underneath it, would only have to stoop the slightest bit.

"It's so high up. How do you get in?"

Sal has been standing back but now he steps forward and unties a rope wrapped around one of the tree trunks, operates the system of counterweights and pulleys that lower the hammock down until she can pat the bottom of it with her flat hand.

"Can I try it?"

She puts a hand on his shoulder; the other clutches the fabric of the hammock. "How do we do this?"

Sal flashes back to the image his mother always liked to tell him about so much – the one where his father picked her up out of the bathtub like she weighed almost nothing at all. Lifted her so easily. Something about that makes Sal swoop Betty up off her feet in a quick graceful motion that makes her give out a small cry. She knew he must be strong but still it catches her off guard. He holds her in his two arms for a moment before lowering her gently down into the hammock.

"Oh," is all she can say as the fabric wraps itself around her.

"Pull me up?" she says. She lies back and Sal operates the ropes, lifts her up into the trees. The hammock begins to sway back and forth a little. She feels herself rising, the evening sky blue and deep where light comes though the green canopy of the boreal forest. She knows she can't be that far off the ground but she's never felt so removed from it. So close to the sky. As though she were floating far above the earth.

"This is wonderful." She shouts the words up into the branches. They flutter down to Sal. She feels a tremendous sense of freedom lying there, swinging lazily back and forth. There's something in it of innocence. Of childhood.

"You must sleep like a baby up here." Then she realizes what she's said and wishes she could take it back. She remembers asking him about his sleep, remembers the way he made a fist, pushed it hard against his temple. She can only imagine the nightmares he's had up here. She's seen the aftermath of them in his eyes.

Sal lowers her back down and before she steps out, takes the hand she puts out for him to take. He helps her to her feet and there's a certain nobility in that for both of them. A certain symbiosis. But her feet have hardly touched down on the forest floor, soft with pine needles, when she looks over his shoulder at something glinting in behind the trees.

"What's through there?" she asks, pointing. Sees a shadow come over his face. There's a path – not the one they came in on – leading off in that direction.

"Where does that go?" she asks again.

His eyes tell her he does not want her to pursue it.

"What is it?" she persists.

He shakes his head the way someone would who had tried and failed to explain something. Failed because it was beyond words.

When Betty begins down the path he rushes up to stop her. Stands before her, shaking his head violently.

"It's okay if you don't want me to. But I'd really like to see it."

She takes another step forward. He puts up his hand.

"Is it a secret? I like secrets. I promise not to tell."

There's a pleading now in his expression that she hasn't seen before. She can't decide what it is he's trying to tell her. What it is he's asking her to do. Not to do. There's something about this hesitation and protest and resistance that tastes different. Something of the need to surrender in it. Not everything about him is telling her to stop. Some part of him is pleading with her to persist. She senses in his body language the need to be conquered. The desire to be overcome. It's as if he wants her to see the very thing he is forbidding her to see. Some deep secret that, by its very nature, longs desperately to be revealed.

When she takes another step forward he backs up, keeps the distance between them constant. And so she takes another, and then another, until she steps into the clearing and sees the menagerie of metal and glass suspended from branches and ropes and chains strung every which way. She puts both hands up to her mouth, tries to breathe. There's something beautiful and terrifying about it. The way all those pieces are hung. The chaotic design of an elaborate child's toy. And yet there is nothing of playfulness in it. Nothing of innocence.

Betty touches a heavy coil spring. Gives it a light push. Then a harder one. It swings back and forth in a long, languid arc until it clangs gently against a steel rod with a muted chime. She wanders through the maze, weaving in and out among the pieces while Sal watches until, from where he's standing, she disappears inside. Then he has to follow her in, afraid that she might really be gone. Lost inside the garden he never wants to visit. Must.

Betty is stepping gingerly between the hanging objects, touching one here, swinging another there, causing small collisions until the forest is chiming and ringing in a way that's different from the sounds Sal hears when he's running through them. In those desperate moments it's a cacophony he's hardly aware of. There's too much going on in his brain. No room to decipher the noise on the inside from the noise on the outside.

"Is this what you do?" she says. "You make music?"

There's no way for him to tell her. And he can't show her. Not now. It wouldn't be anything like the real thing. Because the need is not there now. Won't be, as long as Betty stays. The whole idea of it seems foreign right now. Wrong.

Sal watches her examine a chrome bumper bent into a misshapen curl, all but folded in on itself. Betty rubs at a rust-coloured smudge on the shiny surface. She looks up at him. Moves on to a hard-shell fibreglass fender, the kind that come flying off big rigs when they hit something – a car, a deer. Sal remembers this one because he picked up two or three pieces out of the woods after all the tow trucks and ambulances and police cars had left. The driver must have run off the road after he fell asleep, careened through the ditch and into the trees, the fibreglass shell of the truck cab exploding into a disintegrated mass of splintered shards. Betty is rubbing her fingers across a small stain there. The same colour as the one she just looked at on the bumper. When she looks up at Sal again her expression is darker.

"What are these stains?" she says. "They're all over everything." At first she thought it was paint. But now she suspects that it's something else. "Look. Here." She moves to another piece. "And here. It's blood isn't it? Dried blood. Why is there blood on everything, Sal?"

She moves on to a splintered driveshaft and fingers a shred of fabric clinging to it. "And these." She pulls the cloth free. "There are pieces like this stuck to everything." She moves on to another one hanging from a car hood. Holds it up. "They're all from the same piece of clothing." She holds it up for him to examine. "Is it your coat, Sal? Is that why you weren't wearing it that time you came in? Sal, what do you do in here?" Betty is asking but her eyes are telling Sal that she already knows the answer. The wide-eyed discovery of her revelation terrifies and thrills him at the same time. He wanted this moment. And dreaded it. "This is where you got all those scars and bruises, isn't it Sal? What did you do?" She's asking but not because she hasn't already figured it out. Envisioned this place as a chamber of self-inflicted torture.

Sal feels Betty as a fire drawing him nearer. About to consume him. And somehow he wants to be consumed. Like a night insect about to dive-bomb out of the dark invisible thickness of the midnight air into the glowing embers of the fire with a crackle and hiss – a spark and sputter of death joy. He wants to throw himself into the fire of Betty's revelation, the ecstasy of its end and quick finish, to burn this moment into eternity revealed only in the split second of the hiss hum and crackle roar of that impact. But he can't move. Can only watch as she turns and walks slowly toward him, bringing the fire closer, the dip and curl of the flames licking at his soul.

waiting for elvis

She stands before him now, staring up into his glossy eyes, and takes his large warm hands in hers. Pulls at them until Sal's two outstretched arms are suspended before him. And then – slowly, gently – she steps into the space between them. Waits for them to fold around her.

chapter fourteen

BETTY HAS JUST POURED HERSELF A CUP OF COFFEE when the Greyhound bus, air brakes hissing, pulls into the gravel parking lot of the diner. She can tell right away it's seniors just from the way it takes longer than usual for Harvey to open the door, then a while longer before he appears down the steps. They're taking their time, she guesses, women in their seventies and eighties getting out of their seats, gathering up their sweaters and purses and handbags before they make their way carefully down the aisle to the front of the bus. Harvey's probably brought them straight through from Kenora, started out this morning before the temperature and humidity climbed to where they are now. Days like this, both get up to where you want to run and hide by noon.

The first elderly woman appears at the door of the bus and begins slowly, carefully, to pull herself down the steps with sinewy arms, holding tight to the polished steel rail, bag clutched to her bosom, as though one wrong move will send her plummeting down a precipice. There's nothing wrong with being careful, but Betty can't help thinking that this amount of painstaking prudence is overdone. She feels the urge to run out into the heat and grab the woman. Pry her fingers off the railing. Give her a good shake. Ask her what she is so afraid of. Wrestle her to the ground. Show her how close she really is to it. Pick her up again. Dust her off. Hoist her roughly into the diner. Throw her into a seat. She makes a silent vow never to become someone who gets off a bus like that.

After a few more have made their way down out of the bus in similar fashion, the women steady themselves against each other, arms on the other's shoulders, like some aged and tired post-game soccer players. They head for the diner with a purpose, faces instantly flushed, their physiologies sagging collectively under the ferocity of the heat. When they step into the cool interior of the diner the chatter is of deliverance, as though they have just completed a trek across miles of desert and come to an oasis. Betty steps out from behind the counter to greet them, arranges them in clusters and gets them settled into booths. They bring a cocktail of odours in with them. The smells of talcum powder and diesel fuel and urine all mixed together. The last to come in is Harvey, who takes a stool at the counter.

"Afternoon, Betty," he says, pushing his uniform cap back. "Thought I'd bring you in a load today."

He's been behaving himself ever since Betty gave him the ultimatum. Doesn't give Sal a hard time when he's around. And Betty needs the business.

"Hope you got enough cinnamon buns to go around," he says. "I could do with one myself, if you can spare it. Then I got to go take a hammer to them tires."

The unspoken understanding is that when Harvey brings in a load of seniors like this they will call a truce. And so far it hasn't happened when Sal's been around, so there hasn't really been a problem. But of course he doesn't know what happened at Sal's place in the woods. It would be different if Harvey knew about that. He might not be so friendly.

Betty hasn't seen Sal since that night. He hasn't come around and she hasn't gone out to his place in the woods. Isn't sure she could find it again if she tried. She isn't even sure he'd still be there if she did. Besides, she's decided that he'll come when he's ready. That she can wait as long as it takes. She can't explain what happened. Doesn't see the need. She isn't sure how to feel about it. What to think. The only thing she knows for sure is that it healed something inside her a little. Relieved the sense of longing there for a few short moments. And she thinks maybe it might have done the same for Sal, too. And that's enough.

"How many?" Betty wants to know.

"Small load today. Just seventeen. Maybe the heat kept some of them at home. Can't say I blame them. It's bad out there today. Wouldn't want to be stuck with no air conditioning. Pretty good in here, though." Betty turns it up in the diner now that Arty's not around to scold her for it. Keeps the place nice and cool. If some of the truckers don't like it that's too bad.

"They say it's supposed to get worse before it gets better," says Harvey. "Seeps into the bus on days like this. Wears me out. Comes right through the windows. Up through the floorboards. Turns my stomachs sour. But one of your cinnamon buns should fix that right up."

Harvey is doing all of this talking while Betty busies herself getting out cups and saucers, plates and forks. She's heard all this talk about the heat from the truckers. Harvey's version isn't much different and she isn't really paying attention.

"Heard on the radio people are dying in the city. Old people, mostly. Read in the paper just this morning about this old lady they found dead in her apartment. Found her on the couch in there with all the windows shut up tight."

Betty doesn't want to hear any more of Harvey's conversation. Uses the fact that she has a diner full of seniors to serve as an excuse to stay away from him. If he really wanted to do something for her he could help with the serving, but she knows that isn't going to happen. Whenever he sees how busy she is he starts in on her about hiring some extra help. But Betty doesn't want to do that. Not yet anyway. She wants to try things this way for a while. Wants to feel what it's like to do it all by herself. She's not sure why, except that it's something she needs to get out of her system.

"Turns out she had air conditioning but it was turned off." She's back at the counter and Harvey is still at it. "Imagine that. I figure maybe she just forgot to turn it on. You know how forgetful the old people can be."

Betty heads back out into the diner, but while she pours tea and cuts up cinnamon buns she can't get rid of the nagging possibility that it might be her own mother Harvey is talking about. After all, it's possible Betty might not have heard about it yet. She never did give Ida the new number after she changed it to stop the phone calls. There's no one else, she's sure of that. No brothers or sisters or other relatives to contact. If it was anyone it would have to be her.

But something tells her the woman Harvey's talking about is not Ida. She'd know if it was. Know it inside. Feel it. Her instincts would have told her by now. Just like they tell her that the woman Harvey's talking about probably didn't forget to turn on her air conditioner. That she left it off on purpose. Maybe because she didn't like the loud noise it made, or because she thought it used up too much electricity. Something silly like that. And the old woman hadn't opened a window because she'd seen too many frightening news reports on television. Let herself be intimidated by the nightly newscasts Arty used to watch in bed just before he turned out the lights. Betty could never stand the way they played on people's fears. Always a story about a sexual predator on the loose, or a home invasion, or an assault on a senior. They seemed to Betty like an adult version of a scary bedtime story. The bogeyman for grown-ups.

The old women are busy sipping their coffee and tea, chewing on their cinnamon buns. Most of them probably watch the same kind of newscast on their television sets at night. Betty vows she won't turn out the way they have. Won't end up with their kind of mannerisms, their conversation. She can't help but feel they've abdicated some part of themselves to want to become this way. To make their existence seem so fragile. It's there in the edgy politeness, the shallow empathy they display. Betty had always hoped age would bring her wisdom. But these women do not seem wise to her. Maybe they saved up life too long – until finally they forgot the use of it. Perhaps they lived all their lives under the mistaken assumption that wisdom would come to them as a matter of entitlement, that sheer longevity would automatically bring it about, that they didn't really have to work for it. Maybe they believed that it would arrive simply as a result of all their suffering, sacrifice, submission.

And then, for a moment, Betty wonders whether the old woman Harvey is talking about might have known exactly what she was doing. Sat in her chair with the windows shut and the air conditioning off and just let the heat take her. And that way it would be alright. It wouldn't really be like she was doing anything wrong. Maybe it wasn't relief from the heat she was looking for but relief from life. Perhaps it's possible, Betty thinks, to outlive your own life – to wake up one day and realize it's not so much that you're alive, but that you're just not dead yet. Betty doesn't ever want that to be the last thing she has left to cling to.

Maybe death is like a lot of other things. Maybe it has a best-before date. She wonders what Arty would have been like if he'd made it to old age. What Tony will be like. Whether she will be around to see it. Old herself. Things turned upside down to where dreading her own death is the only thing left to look forward to. Staying alive simply because there's nothing else for her to do.

She's putting down a tray full of tea now, at one of the booths.

"My dear," says one of the women, "you're working so hard. You should get yourself some help." She's fine boned and her fingers are as delicate as the translucent china cup she's holding. Betty ordered in a set of twelve not long ago, just because she knew it would come in handy at times like this. Besides, she likes the feeling of serving up tea in them. It's a nice change from the endless cycle of coffee mugs all day long.

waiting for elvis

"It isn't so bad," says Betty.

"Maybe not now," says one of the other women, "but wait until you get a little older."

"Wait until you get to be our age," says the other one, and pats Betty's arm. "Then you'll see."

"I don't plan on that."

"You don't plan on getting to be this old?"

"No. I meant I don't plan on doing this for that long."

"Of course not. But just the same, you should get some help," says the fine-boned lady, and pats the top of Betty's hand again before she heads back to the counter. Harvey's waiting for her.

"Knew your place would be nice and cool," he says. His hands are up on the counter. He's leaning forward slightly, and Betty prays the coffee will be ready before he works up the nerve to spill out whatever it is he seems to be working up to. "Sure do miss seeing Arty, though."

Betty pulls out a full pot, switches it with an empty one and lets the last of the coffee dribble into it.

"We were all jealous. I guess you probably knew that."

"Jealous? Of this place?"

"Hell no. Not that there's anything wrong with it. I meant you. We always thought Arty was a damn lucky man to have someone like you."

"Someone like me," she repeats. She doesn't know why.

"There's not a man walks into this place doesn't have his eye on you, Betty." She can see now that Harvey has been working himself up to this. That he's really going out on a limb. She pours coffee from the full pot into a line of cups on the tray.

"I always thought Arty didn't appreciate what he had," says Harvey.

She puts the coffee pot back onto the brown circle of the top element.

"I always thought you'd get swept up off your feet by some city slicker that came through here one day. Took one look at you and decided he wanted you for himself. But that never happened. And that's a credit to you, Betty. A real credit. Arty was a lucky man. And that's why, well, when I see you with that. . ."

"Stop right there Harvey."

She gives him a long hard look that says she's waiting for him to say one more thing when the phone rings and Betty slips into the back to answer it. She's been expecting a call. Tony was supposed to get released three days ago. She's hoping this might be the probation officer, asking if she's heard from him. The early parole was none of her doing. It's a hard thing to admit about her own son, but the truth is she figures the longer he stays in there the better. The last time she went to visit him it seemed to her the place might actually be doing him some good. But now he's out and she still hasn't seen or heard from him. He probably got right back into it with that bunch he was hanging around with – Grace and the other two. But he'll come around soon enough when he needs something from her.

"Mrs. Unger?" says the voice at the other end of the line. "Mrs. Betty Unger?"

"Yes. That's right."

"Mrs. Unger, this is Constable Collins of the Winnipeg Police Service. I don't know if you remember me." Just from the tone of his voice Betty can tell it's bad news. And, yes, she does remember him. He was the arresting officer in Tony's case – tall, with a smooth baritone voice and eyes that seemed too kind to belong to a police officer.

"I'm calling about your son. Anthony."

"I know."

"You do? You've already been contacted?"

"Contacted? No, I haven't."

"I see."

"I haven't heard from my son at all."

"Mrs. Unger, you knew your son was released from custody a few days ago?"

"Yes. Don't tell me he's in trouble again already."

"I'm calling to inform you that your son has been admitted to Health Sciences Centre."

waiting for elvis

Betty can't help but feel a small sense of relief. He's injured himself. Smashed up that motorcycle of his. Got beat up in a fight. Anything is better than the alternative.

"I see. He's hurt, then. An accident."

"No. But he's suffered some very serious head injuries."

"Head injuries. How?"

"We're still piecing things together but it looks like your son was the victim of a severe beating."

"A fight? How bad is he?"

"He was unconscious when we found him."

"Found him. Where?"

"It was a house party. We think the assailants were known to him." Betty gets an instant image of Grace in her black leather jacket, smirking through her yellow teeth. "Plenty of drugs and alcohol. We'd already had several calls to the residence. They'd been going at it for a couple of days. We've taken a number of suspects into custody."

"Three of them. Right? A woman and two men. The ones who did this."

"Like I said, we're still piecing things together."

"I know their names. I know who they are."

"We can do all that at another time. I'm sure you want to be with your son, Mrs. Unger."

"Yes. Of course. I'm on my way. Health Sciences, you say?"

"Yes. He's in the intensive care unit."

"Intensive care?" Any relief Betty felt is swallowed by the knot, hard and tight, growing in the pit of her stomach. "How bad is he?"

"When we left the hospital he hadn't regained consciousness. He's listed in guarded condition."

"Guarded condition." There's a long silence while Betty tries to take in the meaning of this. She wasn't prepared for this. Never wanted this. For her boy to be hurt so badly.

"That's correct."

"But he's going to be alright, isn't he?"

"I'm sure they're doing everything they can for your son, Mrs. Unger."

"My son." Betty hears herself say this out loud and the sound of it is different somehow. Something has changed.

"Are you alright, Mrs. Unger? Are you sure you don't want someone to come out and drive you into the city? We can send a patrol car."

"What? No. That won't be necessary, Officer."

"Are you sure?"

"Yes. Yes, I'm fine. Honestly."

"I'm sorry to have to tell you over the phone like this but I thought you'd want to know as soon as possible."

After that things start to fade. First the voice at the other end of the telephone. Next the old women still sitting obediently in their booths, sipping their tea. Chewing on their cinnamon buns. Harvey up at the counter with his coffee cup in his hand. All of it begins to recede into a white fog. Harvey's voice goes from a garble to a muffle to a squeak. Betty sees his body thinning out right before her eyes. The others, too. They are all becoming porous, their bodies disappearing. Their arms and legs, their hands and fingers take on a ghostlike appearance until they are creatures made of nothing more than mist and vapour.

Betty's own body, on the other hand, has never felt so dense. She can feel her heart pumping liquid lead. Her stomach churning steel and iron. Her hands feel like heavy bags of water. Her feet like concrete blocks. And yet she feels the need to flee. To run. Hide. Can't move. It's all she can do just to keep breathing. Thick black tar sticking to the inside of her lungs. She wants to run, literally out of the diner and into the woods, but more than that, she wants to run out of her own skin. Being alive has never felt so heavy.

chapter fifteen

SAL IN HIS HAMMOCK, EARPHONES ON, LISTENING TO the CD player Betty gave him, when something comes seeping in behind the music. It's not the whine and rumble of the highway a few hundred yards away. The intrusion of all that commotion is something he's so used to it's become like the tick tick ticking of the big clock on the wall back home. Something he automatically tunes out. But this is the drone of something else moving out beyond the treeline. Something heavier. Closer. The vibrations are strong enough now to agitate the pointed and delicate tips of the pine trees high above him into an unnatural dance.

The music is something he dug out of a junk pile. He'd found the small plastic case in the ditch months ago, thrown it aside as something he had no use for, but after Betty gave him the player he remembered the case and the picture on the cover. It showed a slight young man wearing a black turtleneck standing in a church before a massive pipe organ. *Daniel Chorzempa Plays Bach* it said. Sal had always wanted to hear a big pipe organ playing. Doesn't remember where he would have got such an idea but it's always been there. When he put the silver disc in and the music started up the rumble and chaos of it rolled all through his body in wave after wave. After that he played it often as he made his way up and down the stretches of highway. It was the best thing he had ever heard to drown out the noise of the traffic.

And now he was letting the music tell a story of sunrise to sunset, of a day like no other. A day without suffering. But this was a day when his body was skin and touch and arousal and all the things he had never felt. Never thought he was entitled to. The music was explaining how Betty washed him from head to toe, down by the river, and how he let himself be washed. Cleansed. How they stood face to face, naked, hand in hand, and knelt on the forest floor where she had spread a blanket made out of their clothes. Took him by the shoulders and gently pulled him down, first over her, then into her. Took him in like he had never been taken. And how they moved. There on the forest floor. He in her. She around him. His hands on her. Hers on him. And how she pulled him deeper again and again until a bursting flood and gush of wordless joy transformed his silence into a cry his body had never uttered before. How it leapt out of him and into the pine-scented air above them.

She looked up at him then, wide-eyed, lifted herself up to kiss him lightly, then a little heavier, on the mouth – legs wide with him still inside – kissed and moved and kissed until she threw her head back in the long wail of a sigh as sweet as anything Sal had ever heard. Would ever hear again.

Sal can taste the memory of it now, lying in his hammock, as an unfamiliar sweetness on his tongue. So different from the bitter aftertaste of the steel fist. This tastes of victory. Of reprieve, however brief, from the tyranny of his daily torture. And he wants nothing more than to lie in his hammock, sway in the breeze, and relive it again and again.

But when the intensity of the noise threatens to overtake the music, Sal can't ignore it any longer and pulls off the headphones, exposing his naked ears to the heavy roar of something menacing the treeline, just beyond the edge of the woods. Sal grabs the rope and lowers the hammock. When he steps out of it and his feet touch the forest floor he feels it moving underneath him. Shaking. Quaking. He can make out something lime green and monstrous between the trees. And then the pines are tilting toward him, toppling and tumbling, falling like shot soldiers. Roots ripped out from under them, they're tossed into a ruined pile, branches snapped and broken, trunks twisted and torn away. The forest is falling in on him. Sal spots another lime-green monster machine, as huge and loud as the other, off to his left. Then another. It's an army of them. The forest is under assault. The invaders crushing everything before them. He can make out someone at the controls of the nearest machine, a scruffy-looking man wearing a white hard hat, and then the only thing Sal can think is that Harry's finally found him. Come for him just like he said he would. All Sal has to do now is look for a row of clothespins along the bill of the hard hat to know for sure, but it's hard to tell from where he's standing. He can make out other men now, at the controls of the other machines, all of them with hard hats on, too. An army of Harries. Pulling levers. Pushing at pedals on the floor. Coming for him.

Off to his left is Sal's shack, and just as one of the machines is about to bulldoze a ruined pine on top of it, the machine stops. The man in the seat waves at the others and the roar dies down to a steady low growl as each one in turn winds down to an idle and the men get off to come and stand next to each other. Sal can hear them shout over the din of the engines.

"What the hell is it?" says one of the men.

"What is that?"

"Where?"

"There."

"Looks like some kind of shack."

"And there. What's all that stuff?"

"Squatters maybe."

"Hunters."

"Could be nothing but a bunch of punk kids that made themselves a fort in the woods."

"You figure?"

"Sure doesn't look like much of a place."

"What about that over there?" One of the men points farther into the woods. "What's all that stuff hanging over there?"

"What the hell?"

"Looks like a bunch of car parts."

"What do you figure they were up to?"

"Some kind of goddamn cult, I bet."

"A gang of those weekend warriors, what-do-you-call-them, militia. Maybe this is where they came to pull their crap. You know. Go out in the bush and shoot their guns off and shit."

"Maybe they use that stuff for target practice."

"You think we should tell Balzer?"

"I'm not telling that asshole one damn thing I don't have to. What he doesn't know won't hurt him."

"He'd probably make us clean this whole goddamn abortion up instead of dozing it down."

"We can just say we didn't see anything."

"It's all crap anyway. I say fuck it."

"I'm with Luke."

"Alright. Enough of this shit. Let's haul balls. But be careful. Don't get that stuff caught up in the tracks. Use the trees to push it down."

Then they're back on their machines and now the trees are coming down hard and fast and there are more lime-green monsters behind them all spewing diesel fumes and heat and Sal feels like maybe the steel fist is in behind them somewhere and runs deeper into the forest. Runs and runs until he comes to the river. Stops to see if he can still hear it. The clamour of all that destruction and chaos. It's quieter now but the noise of tearing and ripping and grinding is still there like some distant herd of enormous creatures consuming everything in their path.

Sal doesn't want to hear it, no matter how far away. He needs total silence. Walks along the riverbank as it winds through the forest and keeps walking until he can sense that it's turned into one of those times when he won't stop for a long time. When the most important thing, the only thing, will be to walk and keep walking. It's been a while since this feeling has come over him, but when it does there's no fighting it. No resisting it. It's like the steel fist that way. Sal can only move. Must move. Eating and sleeping and resting don't matter. Everything recedes. Fades into a background behind other needs, other desires. To hear only the sounds of his own breathing. Feel his limbs propelling him forward. Always forward. Only the sound of his footfalls on the leaves and branches of the forest floor until there's a bridge over the river, but Sal isn't ready to go up onto any road and keeps travelling along the river. Sleeps only when he collapses onto the forest floor in total exhaustion. Wakes and walks again and drinks from the river when he can't ignore the fire of his own thirst. The hunger is easier to ignore but then a stand of mushrooms, pale and succulent, right at his feet and he can't help himself, picks them and eats and then his head is swimming through a rainbow made out of quivering water and the world is stranger than it's ever been.

Sal frozen, the blade of the long knife inches from Clothespin Harry's shiny lizard back, his overalls stretched tight against one of his long, deep sighs. It's time. Sal leaps forward and plunges the knife in. But it catches on a rib and twists, angles off to one side. Before Sal can yank it free and strike again Harry's small hand has struck like a snake and he has Sal by the wrist. Sal lets go and Harry turns slowly, the knife still in his back, to face him.

"Now. What have you done, Big Son? What have you done?" Harry pulls his legs down off the bench and sits up slowly. Makes a face as he straightens up. But his grip on Sal only tightens. He arches his back and turns his head as far as he can to try and get a look at the knife.

"That's a big one," he says. "Now where did you get yourself a knife like that?"

Then he's looking past Sal, at Rosa, who's come around the corner from the kitchen with a wet plate in her hand.

"Rosa, look what your boy's done now." Harry turns stiffly, slowly, until Rosa can see the knife and clutches the plate between her two hands, holds it up over her mouth, eyes wide in terror and disbelief.

"Do you see that, Rosa? Do you see?"

She shakes her head no. Stays against the far wall.

Harry turns slowly back to Sal. *"Now, see what you've done, Big Son? You've gone and upset your mother. It looks like you've learned nothing at all from me and that's a shame. Shove a knife into a man's back. Stick him like pig. It's a disappointment."*

Sal understands that it wasn't far enough to reach Clothespin Harry's beating heart. That it needed to go deeper. Harry lets go of Sal and reaches around awkwardly, one arm, then the other, fingertips reaching for the handle, to see if he can get hold of the knife. *"You've done a damn dirty thing here, Big Son. When did I ever do anything like this to you?"* The words are coming slower and more deliberate now. Harry's taking short quick breaths in between. *"Tell me. When did I ever hurt you like this?"*

A small trickle of blood appears at the corner of Harry's mouth. He licks at it with his tongue. Dabs at it with the tip of one small finger. Inspects the finger. *"Now as soon as I get this knife out of my back I'm going to have to hurt you back. You understand that, don't you?"* He coughs, politely puts a curled fist up to his mouth. *"And it'll have to be different this time. This time I'm going to have to open you up. Now let me just sit here for a minute and figure this out. I just need some time. That's all."*

Sal understands what he means. Clothespin Harry needs time to figure a way he can kill them both. He can see from the terror in his mother's eyes that she believes him. And Sal believes him, too. The knife is deep in Harry's back, but there's almost no blood where it went in. He should have known it was never going to be so simple. Should've known Harry wouldn't allow himself to be killed so easily.

Clothespin Harry moves forward a little, groans with the effort, until he's sitting on the very edge of the wooden bench. All the blood has left his face. *"I have to tell you that's damned uncomfortable."*

Rosa walks slowly and carefully over to stand next to Sal. Grabs his shoulders in a fierce grip. Lowers him down onto the ratty couch, then sits down beside him. Sal looks over at her. She's watching Harry, and the look on her face is a little like the times she'd be sitting in the Walhalla Theatre, waiting for Elvis. Only now she's as

waiting for elvis

pale as Harry. Sal and his mother sit side by side and watch. The only sound for a long time is the ticking of the clock on the wall. He's leaning a little farther forward now, a hand on one knee. Rivulets of milky sweat are running down his temples, beading up on his forehead. One girlish hand reaches along the bench, feeling for his hard hat. When he finds it he places it slowly and delicately on his head. Tucks it into place. He opens his mouth and it looks like he wants to say something but no words come out. There's no way to predict what's coming. Harry might fall over on his side, or collapse onto the floor, or he might get up and cross the room and kill them both with his bare hands.

"He's figuring a way to kill us now," says Sal.

"No, Sal. Not both of us. Time has come. You have to go."

"Where?"

"Out that way." Rosa indicates the side door of the shack.

"And you can't ever come back."

"Never?"

"Never."

"But maybe I killed him and he's just taking his time dying and all we have to do is wait."

"We can't take that chance."

"What if I go and wait in the woods for a while and then come back. How would that be?"

"No, Sal."

"Or we could both go. Take the pickup truck."

"No."

"But why, Rosa?"

"Because it has to be just you. Like I said all along. Just you. Remember everything we talked about? Well, now is the time. He's weak, Salazar. He won't come after you. Not with that knife in his back. You stuck it deep, Sal. Deep. You hurt him. So when you get up now you walk slow and easy to that door and keep walking right through it and don't stop. Not for anything. Understand? I'll keep him here. I can handle him now. You remember what I told you, don't you? Tell me you remember."

"I remember."

"Head east, like I told you."

"But what'll happen to me?"

"I can't say, Sal, honey. But you have to do it just the same. It's the only way. Harry can't hurt you now." In all of this Rosa never once takes her eyes off Clothespin Harry's. Keeps them fixed on his.

"Then come too."

"I can't do that."

"Yes, you can. We can both go."

Harry is swaying now, ever so slightly, from side to side. One hand has come up as if it were floating in front of him, fingers curled, palm down, reaching for something.

"I have to stay here."

"But why?"

"Because I have to. Because I have to know."

"Know? Know what?"

"I can't explain it. I don't know if I understand it myself. Now kiss your mother goodbye." Rosa doesn't turn her head. Keeps her eyes fixed and steady strong on Harry's, the two of them engaged in some kind of contest Sal's not part of. He gets up and leans forward, kisses his mother on one cold cheek.

Then, without ever turning her head, she says calmly and quietly, "You go now, Salazar. Go to the door. It's alright. I've got him. And remember. You're my best and only hope. You always will be. My best and only hope."

Sal gets up and walks slowly toward the door. Waits for Harry's eyes to follow him but they don't. The two of them, Harry and Rosa, sit staring across the room at each other like they're both in some kind of trance. Hypnotized. Immobilized. The last thing Sal sees is Rosa with her two hands clasped between her knees, as if she were holding on to something there. Harry with his hand out, palm curled up now, as if to catch something falling from the ceiling.

chapter sixteen

BETTY LIGHTS A CIGARETTE, TAKES IT OUT OF HER mouth and sticks it carefully in between Tony's lips. He pulls hard and long until the tip glows fiery red, then parts his lips slightly and inhales deeply, holds the smoke there for a long time before he lets out two long streams, one through his nose and another through his mouth. The two streams cross each other and mingle in the still of late evening, clouding the air around his head in a white fog.

The nurse will be coming by soon to wheel him inside and get him ready for bed, but just now the two of them are alone on the porch, Betty sitting on a wicker chair next to her ruined son. She often sits like this with him, in silence, enjoying the last of the sun. That seems to be the time Betty likes to come – she isn't sure why. Maybe it has something to do with the way Sal used to come around, just before she closed the diner. Back there she always thought of it as the best time of the day, when the earth and sky didn't seem all that different from each other, when the light above the trees was at its most benevolent, and the air its most fragrant. There's always been something of surrender and acceptance about a sunset for Betty. The day is almost over. No need to get too upset about what's to come. For all these reasons

waiting for elvis

she often seems to end up here around that time of day. It's not like she doesn't have the time now that the diner's gone.

Tony pulls in another mouthful of smoke and the end of the cigarette glows brighter, the bent cylinder of ash dips further down, about to fall weightlessly into his crumpled lap. White smoke curls up around his pale eyes. Betty watches him try to intensify the expression that's always been second nature to him: the snarl and scowl of his dissatisfaction. But now, thanks to the damage his nervous system and musculature have suffered, what materializes instead is a look of benign indifference.

Inside, Betty knows he must still be trying to come to terms with his crippled existence. His first fierce attempts at roaring, fresh out of the hospital, when he saw only through the red filter of his rage, have mellowed down to a slow, steady glow of resentment much the same as a stubborn animal that finally ceases bellowing out the injustice of its captivity and settles into a brooding silence that carries it through the long dumb hours of another day, a week, a year. It doesn't help that he's lost the ability to speak. When he tries, not much more than garble comes up from deep in his throat. The brain damage is so severe it will not allow him more control of his vocal cords than a few indecipherable expectorations. They manifest themselves as little more than drools of spittle down his chin and an erratic bobbing of his cigarette up and down as he tries desperately to make himself heard. Now, out of his broken body, a steady glumness oozes, thinly, out of every pore, like oil onto a snake's skin. Gives him his sheen, his slick patina of ennui.

Betty knows her son's entire universe has been shattered, but she also understands the hard truth that it never consisted of much more than a collection of petty defeats and victories within a hundred mile radius of where they're sitting now. The same might be true for her. For a lot of people. The difference is that now, when she comes to visit him like this, sit with him on the porch, light his cigarettes, his condition allows for possibilities that never existed before. For her, his crumpled body is the best thing that ever happened between them.

waiting for elvis

It started with the realization that she would never have to watch her son go to prison again. There would be no more trials. No more sentences. No more jail time. He wasn't going anywhere like that ever again. Tony's jailor from now on would be his own body. He would live out his life here, at this acute-care facility, where they can give him the twenty-four-hour-a-day supervision he needs. She was not prepared for the tremendous relief this gave her.

When he first regained consciousness and figured out what had happened to him, she could see in his eyes the confusion and rage. He was like a wounded dog that refused to let itself heal. Wanted to bite into the place where it hurt again and again – inflict pain on its own flesh. A creature that could not fathom the notion of leaving off for the sake of its own healing. Her son never did know how to endure suffering, only how to inflict it – even if only upon himself. But that is not an option now.

She has Grace and her two buddies to thank for this, but by the time the police called her in to explain what had happened, Betty wasn't really interested in hearing it. Still, she'd listened politely while the officer across the desk from her told her how, based on eyewitness accounts, three assailants had tried to beat her son to death. A drunken argument had broken out at a party, then a fight that spilled outside the house. When the police arrived on the scene they discovered Tony, bloody and unconscious, next to his kicked-over motorcycle. He ended by telling her about the arrests that had been made and the charges laid against Grace, as well as Carl and Eddy.

She didn't want to listen to much of it because she'd known from the beginning that sooner or later Grace would turn on Tony, just as she'd known that her son would have turned on her eventually – on anyone. Everyone. Even himself. They were the same that way. One a reflection of the other. While the officer spoke and Betty nodded she found herself imagining the situation the other way around, not sure how to feel about it.

Now she fishes a shiny plastic case out of the paper bag she brought with her. She has to untangle the earphones and forgets about the cigarette in Tony's mouth until she hears him trying to spit it out, looks up, quickly pulls the stub from between his lips and butts it in the ashtray resting on the railing of the porch, then carefully places the small black case in Tony's concave lap.

"It's your CD player," she says. "Remember? The one you gave me before you went away. I don't have any of the CDs you used to play. I think I might have thrown them out. But there's already one in here I thought you could listen to." The CD player is the one she gave Sal. She found it, still intact, with his favourite CD inside, the one with the organ music. The fact that he didn't take it with him is still a mystery to her. She can't decide whether it was deliberate – that he meant for her to find it – or whether he was just in too much of a hurry when he left.

She'd found it that day she finally decided to go back there – first to the diner, then to Sal's place in the woods. She hadn't planned on staying away so long. At least she didn't think she had. She'd meant to go back sooner. If only for Sal's sake. And, yes, for hers. But the days and nights at Tony's bedside had bled into each other until they became indistinguishable. Time became fluid and arbitrary until days turned into weeks and still she had not gone back. But there was always a part of every day when she found herself thinking about Sal. Imagined him walking out of the woods at dusk in his greatcoat, crossing the empty parking lot only to find the door still locked, the Closed sign up, the diner dark and deserted. Pictured him wandering back to his place in the woods alone.

But this thing that kept her at her son's bedside, this wasn't guilt. And it wasn't fear. She understood that deep down her son Tony did not really deserve what she was going to give him. But she wasn't going to do it for him. She was going to do it for herself. She was going to indulge herself in all the things a mother wants to do for a son and hasn't been allowed to. A selfish act of gratification. He was going to have to let her do what she'd always wanted to, always needed to, as his mother. And there was nothing he could do to stop her. It was a bittersweet feeling because she hated to see him so hobbled, but loved the possibilities it had opened up. A lot of the time she didn't know what to think about how it felt. She only knew that she couldn't get enough of it.

It began in the hospital room, when she saw how deeply her son was suffering. A few quick tears came, before she could stop them, when she walked into the room and saw him lying on the bed, hooked up to all those machines by a tangle of tubes and wires. Right then and there something began to change in her. And even after the doctors hinted he might have slipped into a coma he would never come out of, the feeling only grew, only increased, even after they told her that if he did regain consciousness the swelling and haemorrhaging in his brain were so severe there was sure to be significant impairment – certainly physical, possibly mental.

She would sit next to his bed in the semi-darkened room, take his hand in hers, listen to him breathe. She knew his needful inhalations were only the involuntary workings of his deep unconscious, but the sound of them was unlike anything she'd ever heard from her son. She remembered back to the times when he was a child and she'd slipped next to his bedside in the middle of another sleepless night to listen to the deep sleep of her tired young boy. How his breathing had always sounded so restless to her, as if, even in his dreams, he was still at war with the world. But, watching her son's chest rise and fall as he lay on the hospital bed, what she heard seemed more like a plea.

And over the course of the next days and weeks, all the barricades Betty had erected began to come down. All the ways she'd hardened herself began to soften. And she had Grace to thank for it. Grace had killed the part of her son that had always gotten in the way before. Crippled his ability to assault her with his anger, his need. And now, thanks to Sal, something oddly therapeutic was emerging out of that paralysis. It was Sal who'd taught her a different way of being with someone. A quiet way. And so, for the first time in her life, Betty realized that it might be possible to love her son after all. Love him – with his broken spirit, his ruined body – in a way she never could when he was whole. A part of him had been murdered, but perhaps it was just what was needed to save the rest. She understood all of this because she had learned it from Sal. Realized what he must have been trying to do each time he made himself run through his hanging garden, threw himself against all that jagged metal and glass until he'd bludgeoned himself into unconsciousness. He had been trying, the only way he knew how, to murder a part of himself – the part he couldn't live with.

And somewhere in there she came to contemplate the possibility that perhaps all of them – Sal and Tony and Ida and she, herself – would stay broken. That they could never be fixed. And if it was true, if there was no way for them to climb out of so much rubble and chaos, perhaps the best thing was just to find a way to live in the ruins. And so she stayed at his bedside night and day, drinking in all the new possibilities, until one evening she tore herself away to drive out to the diner. When she went to put the key in the lock there were three pieces of paper, one blue, one green, one red, taped to the door. She took them down and brought them inside with her to read. They were notices from the Manitoba Department of Highways, written in bureaucratic legalese. She read as far as " . . . provides that where an authority may apply to the Municipal Board to prescribe, and the Board may prescribe, the terms and conditions, including the provision of other lands and facilities, upon which the expropriation may proceed" and didn't bother with the rest. There was a telephone number at the bottom for her to call and the name of a person to contact.

At first Betty was relieved at the idea she'd never have to open the place up again, but then it struck her that if the highway was coming through they might already have started. She wondered just how close they were. Thought of Sal's place in the woods. Ran down the trail, worried she would take a wrong turn and end up lost, until she stumbled out into the open where the forest should still have been. Saw the clear-cut timber, the lime-green bulldozers and scrapers parked for the night in a line along the trees.

She made her way across the uneven and ugly terrain, to a dishevelled ridge of branches and limbs, roots and dirt all pushed up against the edge of the forest where she could make out the ropes and cables and pieces of plastic and metal in among the debris, and she knew she was looking at what was left of Sal's garden of torture. She could see the remains of the shack he'd built, too, and thought everything had been destroyed until she remembered the hammock a little farther in, climbed over the ridge and there, in the trees behind it, still swinging in the breeze, was the hammock, untouched, and nestled inside it, the CD player – as if Sal had carefully placed it there for her to find.

Now Betty takes up the two earphones and carefully inserts one in each of Tony's ears. He's looking up at her, unable to muster much of a change in expression. The way the doctors explained it to Betty, his facial muscles, like the rest of his body, don't really respond to the neural commands his brain tries to give them. Mostly the signals get lost along the way. Detoured. Blocked. Turned back. But Betty has learned to read his eyes, just as she learned to read Sal's. Her son's eyes tell her that not a lot has changed inside, that it's only the physical manifestations which are different. There has been no courageous act of will to raise himself above his handicap, ascend to a higher plane of daily existence. No epiphany that will help him become a better person.

Still, there's time for that. Lots of time. Eventually, perhaps, some small seedlings of courage may sprout. Some tiny spores of humility may germinate. And when they do Betty will be there to nurture them. True, there's a lot that can never be overcome. Never forgotten. Never fixed. But now that Tony's body is broken, he will have to allow himself to be accessed. For the first time in his life, he will not be able to stop Betty from loving him. All his old ways of pushing her away are not going to be available to him. And she is not afraid of his silence, his lack of response. It doesn't intimidate her in the least. She learned from

waiting for elvis

Sal how to appreciate the openness of being able to speak to someone who will not answer you.

When Betty sat with him those first few days and nights, her hand over his, she loved the freedom of that. Freedom to whisper words close to his ear, brush his cheek. She could feel him fighting his way back from death. Using all of his strength to keep it at a distance, in the same way he had always kept her at a distance. There were times when death was so close she could feel it hovering in the air, up near the ceiling. Squatting on top of the small grey television set suspended there. Waiting. Waiting for her son to lose his will. But in the end it was Tony's anger that kept him fighting. Allowed him to live. Those were the nights when she would sit next to him, listen to the battle his heart and lungs and muscles were putting up, sense how much it was taking out of him, how much it was costing him, and weep silently. For him. For herself. In those semi-dark hours, listening to the hum and beep of hospital machinery, the distant noises of trays and squeaky running shoes and switchboards, Betty sometimes wept to think that she and all the people closest to her lived in such silent, separate worlds.

When Betty places the CD player on Tony's lap, he leans his head a little sideways, as if to make inserting the earphone a little easier. When they're in place she pushes the Play button. The player still has the same disc in it Sal always had. Daniel Chorzempa playing Bach. By now she's familiar with the piece he would listen to over and over. "Passacaglia and Fugue in C Minor." It's not the kind of music she would have sought out on her own, but since she found the player in his abandoned hammock that night and brought it back home with her, she's been playing it, usually after she gets into bed for the night. She turns the volume up until the low vibrations of the organ rumble through her chest. And when the final chord, endless and mighty, rolls in like a warm wave, she imagines how it must have bathed Sal's body, healed his soul.

And she's thinking now that perhaps the music can evoke some of the same feelings in Tony. The kind of thing no language, no spoken word can articulate. Perhaps it can speak all the things her son cannot. What it means to be alive, breathe in the notes, feel himself elevated for a moment. Raised up. Lifted. Betty imagines the music taking her son up onto the tips of his toes, then up off the ground. Floating him up out of his wheelchair, out from under the eaves of the porch, over the crowns of the shady elms, up into the clouds.

She watches his reaction. Understands that the rhythmic swaying of his head from side to side, as if he were moving to the music, cannot be trusted. The doctors have told her that the neurotransmitters in her son's spine are unable to convey successfully much information to his muscles. So it's just as possible he might be trying to shake his head violently, desperate to dislodge the earphones. That it's the best he can manage. But she's already decided that it really doesn't matter. From now on she's going to give herself permission to decide what's good for her son. From now on, he will have to allow her liberties always denied to her before.

One of the attendants walks by pushing a cart full of trays. She smiles at Betty. Her name is Imelda. Like most of the staff, she takes an efficient, businesslike approach to looking after Tony's needs. Treats him the way she would treat any other patient. Performs each act of cleaning, wiping, grooming, with magnificent disinterest. Tony's early attempts at abusing her have been futile. If he tries to spit on her, he only succeeds in dribbling down the front of his shirt. If he soils his pants deliberately, rather than waiting for help, he only ends up sitting in his own filth. He has begun to accept that from now on he will have to make do with only the smallest doses of self-gratification – his intermittent cigarettes, his humiliating feedings and evacuations.

The staff are efficient, but rough. Their attention to his level of comfort or discomfort remains constant, if only just adequate. They change and clean and dress him as though his body were simply flesh that needs to be managed. He's had to come to grips with what it feels like to be manhandled. Betty knows this must have been hard for him, since it was always he who did the manhandling, he who exulted in the feeling of domination over the physical commodities of his fellow human beings. And now, suddenly, it's all been turned on its head.

Betty is thinking about how much Sal taught her. How words really aren't necessary a lot of the time. How it can all be much simpler than that. How most things people say don't need saying. Are better left unsaid. A lot of the time there's more reason not to talk than to talk. A lot of the time what people say isn't really like talking at all. It's something else. A call. A cry from the most needful of creatures.

And it will have to be the same with her mother. There will be no more visits to the decrepit apartment for more recrimination. More bile. Betty has already made plans for her mother's future. They will be carried out without Betty subjecting herself to her mother's protests. Her rants. She's signing the papers tomorrow and then her mother will be taken, by force if necessary. Sent to dry out. After that Betty is having her placed in a home where she can live out the rest of her days. It's all been arranged without Betty having any contact. She knows to an outsider it must seem cruel but it has to be done that way. All those nights in the quiet hospital room gave her time to think, helped her come to the conclusion that sometimes, between a mother and daughter, a mother and son, the time comes to forgo the fruitless hopes for penitence, for redemption. To opt instead for cold detachment. For something that, to an outsider, looks a lot like cruelty. She's come to understand that from now on she must allow herself the cruelty to give the people she loves what they most need in spite of themselves. And in all of this, words are not important. Words only get in the way.

It's time for Tony to go inside now, and as she watches Imelda wheel him away, she knows she'll be back tomorrow. And the next day. Her son needs her now. She can finally be of use to him. And Sal has taught her so much that she can use. Day by day, Tony will have to make himself a little more available to her. The urgency of his need to distance himself from her will fade. She will get closer. The deep canyon between them can never be crossed, but the far side is just a little more visible now.

When she gets to the exit that will take her back to Hayden, to the house she will soon be putting up for sale, instead of making the turn, she drives on, continues along the highway. It's one of those endless summer evenings when light lingers in the northern sky long after sunset, so there's time. They've torn the diner down by now, Betty's sure, and she needs to see what that looks like – for the place not to be there. Now that Sal's gone, it's important that the diner should be gone as well. And this will be her way of bearing witness to the absence of both.

She knows she's close when the place where the divided used to end becomes, instead, two lanes of fresh blacktop that cut through a still-raw corridor of spruce and pine forest. She continues on through the dusk, slows down when she thinks she must be near the place, not sure whether she's passed it or not. She parks along the shoulder, gets out and walks down the slope and into the wide, barren ditch, toward the forest. Stops halfway. Takes a few steps one way, then the other. Tires and engines scream by up on the new highway. She begins to search the ground for clues. Here and there the first few thistles and clumps of quack grass have begun to sprout up out of the disembowelled earth. But already, along with the strands of roots and clumps of dirt, fast-food containers and beer bottles and dirty shreds of rubber tires can be found. Then her attention is caught by something in the dirt. She stoops to pick up a shredded triangle of faded green plywood, recognizes it instantly as a small corner of the sign that Arty put up over the diner when they first got the place.

She curls her fingers around it, clutches the piece in her hand. Gazes, long and deep, into the darkening woods. And just for a moment, before she turns away, allows herself to imagine a man in a greatcoat, somewhere next to another forest, along a different stretch of road.

epilogue

Sal, at the edge of the forest, looking past the traffic at something far out in the lake. It's been days and days of nothing but forest and shoreline and the highway that runs between them. Today the waves washing up on the rocky shoreline are loud enough to hear when there's a brief lull in the roar of the traffic. He can't remember how long he's been walking. Where he started from. But he's heading east, like Rosa said to. He's been waiting for the highway to turn south but the lake won't let it. Just goes on and on, like an ocean. And so he follows. Living on scraps out of fast-food bags and boxes he picks up out of the dirty weeds and brush and grass next to the road. Sleeping on pine boughs thrown together on the forest floor a few yards in from the treeline.

The last few days the breeze off the lake has had an edge to it. It's coming winter and nights are cooler now but still his coat keeps him warm. The one she gave him. Betty. That was her name. Something about a light from a window in the middle of the endless forest. A booth. A table and her across from him sipping at a cup. But that must have been another place, another highway.

Sal has stopped long enough to try and get a better look at something out on the deep blue water. Something swimming, strong and tireless, across the whitecapped waves. It's been there every day when he looks out, heading in the same direction he's walking. Stays even with him. Never rests. And always just far enough out from the shore so he can't quite make it out. Might be animal. Might be human.

The steel fist still hovers on days like this but the crippling flashbacks have all been distilled into one that repeats and repeats.

Sal dreaming out the window of Clothespin Harry's pickup, staring over at the window of the toy store. He'd like to go in and see all the toys and games but Harry told him to wait in the truck like always while he and Rosa drink in the bar across the street. It seems to Sal they've been in there a couple of hours now but it's hard to tell. It might have been longer. Sometimes a whole day will pass, afternoon to evening to nighttime, and Sal has to open the door a crack so he can relieve himself, and try to sleep on the uneven seat but never really sleep because Harry might crash open the door at any moment and see him lying there asleep and say, "You were supposed to keep an eye out, Big Son. That'll cost you."

But this time Sal can't help himself and steps out of the truck and inside the store and walks between the aisles looking into bin after bin of the little toy trucks and tanks and soldiers and dolls and Sal wants them all and knows he can't have even just one. Trinkets and bracelets, too, and a pretty girl in a yellow summery dress with shiny long hair and such smallness in her features. She's looking at a glistening bracelet of glass beads and Sal would like to buy it for her. Slip it over her hand and around her wrist. She has delicate wrists, the girl. She turns her pretty head and looks at him standing there, staring at her.

"What's your name?" she asks.

"Salazar."

"That's a nice name."

She looks like she is about to say something else but just then the girl's mother appears around the corner. She looks over at Sal, hurries to take her daughter by the hand and leads her away. The girl tries to drop the bracelet back into the bin before she's pulled away but it misses and falls to the floor with a harsh jangle. Glass and beads scatter. Sal picks up a few of the pieces. Cradles them in his palm.

They have their backs to him now. The mother leans over and he hears her say, "What were you doing with that boy?"

"Nothing," the girl answers. "I wasn't doing anything."

"You mustn't ever let a boy like that near you. Do you understand?"

"He seems nice."

"He's filthy."

"He looks alright to me." The girl tugs her hand out of her mother's.

"Did you see his clothes? His hair?"

The mother disappears around the corner of the aisle but the girl stops for a moment. Her mother calls to her, puts her hand out and takes the girl by the wrist.

"Elizabeth. For heaven's sake, come on."

But just before she disappears around the end of aisle, the girl turns to look over at Sal, and even as her mother leads her out of sight, she smiles. And Sal has never felt so small and so big.

He looks down at the pieces of the bracelet still in the palm of his hand. They shimmer. They glow. They shine.

acknowledgements

THANKS TO Edna Alford and Geoffrey Ursell for their insight and suggestions, and to Robert Kroetsch for his editorial input early on. With special appreciation for my wife, Brenda Sciberras. Thanks, also, to the Manitoba Arts Council for their support.

about the author

DAVID ELIAS is the author of three other books, the novel *Sunday Afternoon* and the short story collections *Places of Grace* and *Crossing the Line*. His work has also appeared in many journals and periodicals in Canada and the US. His short story "How I Crossed Over," from *Places of Grace* was a finalist for the 1995 Journey Prize. He holds a degree in philosophy from the University of Manitoba and divides his time between teaching and writing. He currently lives and works in Winnipeg where he is active in the Winnipeg Philharmonic Choir.

Other Coteau Books by David Elias:

PLACES OF GRACE:
In a sheltered valley paradise in southern Manitoba, a community of Mennonites has tried to insulate itself from the rest of the world, following the strictest traditions of culture and religion. But they cannot entirely escape the pressures of the outside world.

SUNDAY AFTERNOON:
One day during the Cuban missile crisis, the Manitoba Mennonite village of Neustadt confronts a crisis of its own – the return of bombshell Katie Klassen, now a Hollywood movie star.

Available at fine bookstores everywhere.
WWW.COTEAUBOOKS.COM